the floodmakers

also by mylène dressler

The Deadwood Beetle

The Medusa Tree

· *the* ·

floodmakers

MYLÈNE DRESSLER

G. P. Putnam's Sons
New York

This is a work of fiction. Names, characters, places, and incidents either are the product of the author's imagination or are used fictitiously, and any resemblance to actual persons, living or dead, business establishments, events, or locales is entirely coincidental.

G. P. Putnam's Sons
Publishers Since 1838
a member of
Penguin Group (USA) Inc.
375 Hudson Street
New York, NY 10014

Published simultaneously in Canada

Library of Congress Cataloging-in-Publication Data

Dressler, Mylène, date.
The floodmakers / Mylène Dressler.
p. cm
ISBN 0-399-15163-X
I. Title.
PS3554.R432F57 2004 2003058021
813'.54—dc22

Printed in the United States of America
1 3 5 7 9 10 8 6 4 2

This book is printed on acid-free paper. ∞

Book design by Stephanie Huntwork

FOR MY FAMILY

Can't I just as well say "the depths of the sea"?

Yes, but it sounds so strange to me when someone else says "the depths of the sea."

—IBSEN, *The Wild Duck*

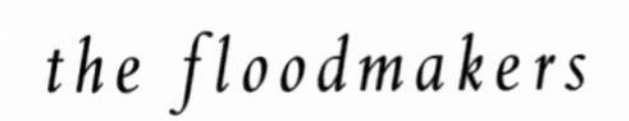
the floodmakers

· 1 ·

The buffer between New York and Texas is slighter than sand, it's so easily breached. That morning I picked up the telephone to hear Mama—I very rarely, that is my sister and I both very rarely call our second mother by her first name, which is Jean—raising her voice over the barking dogs and the excited castaneting of crawfish boiling on the stove.

"Now Harold," she said.

"Harold" sounds formal when you've just nearly drowned.

"I can tell you, since we're all settled in at the Gulf again," I heard her scrape and bang something against a pot, "it's been decided. Your father says he's not going to put up with anymore crank medical interference."

My father, at eighty-one, sometimes confused being a retired playwright with being a retired director of cardiology.

I held my wet forehead in my hand, leaned over the desk, and let my bathrobe loosen and my knees give over the sides of the chair, my chin sloppy on the receiver, my ear sinking in close enough to hear the moaning of the surf on the other side.

"You mean," I said as normally as I could for someone who's just woken up in his bathtub, "he's not going to take any of his pills, anymore?"

"No, dear. Well—only the diuretics. He says that's enough. He says he's fed up with all the rest. He says the tests are imprecise, that they exaggerate the, the *motives* of the disease."

"Which are—?"

"You know, he says it doesn't want to kill him. It's just *preparing* him."

I'd grown up with this sort of thing. A full thirty-six years' worth. I didn't even have to acknowledge the aside. I just squeezed my eyes shut to get some control over the stinging, and then opened them again. "So, no more beta-blockers."

"That's right, dear." I heard her rattle what sounded like a steel lid, then some muffled turning away to say something short and shooing to their terriers, Willie and Able. "He said," she came back on, her voice sounding even gruffer and lower than usual, "those things were making him so fuzzy, he couldn't think."

And then some smothered rustling; and she let out half a cough, half exhausted sigh.

Well that's odd, I thought, still in a drugged fog.

Mama, Jean, former East Coast Ladies Champion, never sounded tired.

"Mama—you all right down there?"

"Now, dear," she drawled. "Why *wouldn't* I be?" A slight grunting. Some heaving, as though she were picking up a ten-pound roast in one hand. "My bones are coming along just fine, since you want to know. Everything's under control. A flea on a leash."

"And how were Daddy's doctors this time?"

"You do remember how the last visit went."

Insults. Charges of incompetence. A blood-pressure cuff he'd ripped from his arm like rejected rank.

"Although that younger one, you remember, Harry, the one I told you about? He did try putting on his *meanest* game face. But still, when it came down to actually talking to your father, he folded like another duffer in front of the clubhouse. Then afterwards he had to the nerve to come over and try and lecture *me—outside* the examining room, mind you now, the chicken! 'Ma'am' "—and here she lowered her voice to a hoarse whisper—" 'he just better learn to take it *easier,* because this next three months is going to be very, very important.' "

As if my eighty-one-year-old father were only sweating out a difficult pregnancy. As though all he had to do, for the first time in his life, was keep quiet, and lie on his back, calmly, and he might be able to carry his fisted, congested heart to term.

"Harry, honey? You there? You all right?"

"Yes, Mama." My hair was still dripping.

"You sure? No problems, not with a new play, or anything? Nothing wrong at home?"

"Not at the moment."

"Well, then. If that's the case." The invitation in her voice was slanted, but clear.

"All right, Mama. What are you thinking?"

"Nothing, dear! Just mulling over a nice weekend. I do need to get out of doors a bit, I don't know how you're feeling?"

She had been a star in her own right. With my father's poor health, though, she'd been cooped up more than she liked.

"So you do want me to come down, Mama."

"Oh. Well now."

"It's all right. It's not a problem. I can get on a plane." I could, I realized. Tomorrow. Today. No one was keeping me, or maybe a better way to put it would be, I was keeping no one. Look at you, a gay man in a plaid robe. Tim would have wrinkled his nose. It's like a chow wearing a bandanna.

"Of course, Harry, you know how much we *hate* interrupting you kids' private lives."

"Mama."

"I mean it, dear. You know I do."

"I know, Mama."

"It's not like there's anything to worry about."

"Mama?"

"Well. All right then."

And that had been the second unusual thing. Jean, Mama, didn't usually throw her game that quickly.

"We've got Sarah coming down too," she added brightly. "With Paul."

"Guess she wants to take a look at Daddy herself?"

"Guess you could put it that way. Not that there's anything to worry about. Not at all. I want you both to know that."

Of course not. Nothing was ever upsetting in my family. That would mean—getting upset. "I just hope, Ma, they're not bringing their camera down with them again."

"She did say she was planning to get in a few more shots. You know how these cineastes are."

But my sister had only recently become a filmmaker. Before that she'd been, in casual succession, a sculptor, a yoga instructor, an installation artist (working with foam and cardboard), a tattoo designer, an art gallery partner, and a "specialty leather consultant." The last time we'd seen each other, on the Fourth of July, at the big house, she'd pushed her freckled nose up close to mine and whispered she'd finally realized: there was no point in our having our nice tidy little trust funds if we weren't going to go out and do something really *noble* with the cash—like make documentaries. My poor baby sister. She actually thought she was documenting Daddy, who morphed from a sly fox into a living saint the minute the lens cap popped off.

"And I'll bet," I wiped my dripping forehead, "Daddy said all right to another interview."

"He does like to help his little chickadees out."

"I know that," I managed to keep the sarcasm out of my voice. "I just thought that little project was all finished now."

"I don't know about that, dear. I guess, sometimes, it's hard to know exactly when a thing *is* finished. Anyway," she went on hurriedly, "you know how all you *men* are, when you get older." And she coughed away from the phone and let out another low, muscular laugh. The sound of it, though, perfectly well behaved. Always, always, in spite of her voice, and what was left of those hulking forearms, carefully ladylike, was Mama. "Do you know, he told me just last week it was high time he paid more attention to his *visual* legacy?"

"Probably because of that PBS interview."

She interrupted me shortly. "Anyway. Since you don't have anything else on, you *will* hurry up and get down here?"

And that impatience had been the third odd thing. Because Mama, Jean Dugan, former professional, was never jumpy. A long-distance putting champ, a player who in the 1950s had driven farther and more accurately than it was thought proper women *could* drive—she knew how, when she wanted, to keep her hands steady, her steely gaze pointed.

But then, I thought, putting the phone down and wiping the last of the bathwater and the sleeping pills away from my eyes, why expect anyone—especially a crawfish-boiling, distracted, seventy-one-year-old arthritic—to be able to hit on anything through a hole as small as a phone jack?

· 2 ·

The rain pounded down on the hood of my rental in a shifting, diamond-backed pattern. Downtown Houston disappeared from my rearview mirror. Farther out, the latest suburbs had bulldozed everything aside: gone were the white geese that this time of year used to pick through the soggy rice fields, back when there were rice fields, back when we used to make this trip of three hours, on weekends and holidays, or the spur of the moment, whenever my father needed to, whenever he sighed and said the city was just too hot and too crowded a place to land the albatross of Great Theater.

Mama and the great Babe Zaharias had once played a tournament in the glut of a downpour like this one. (But then, you know, Mama had explained it to us, you know how it *was,* back in those days, when we were really struggling to get the women's pro tour going, and trying to prove we were ladies and champions, too—we would do just about *anything* to get people's attention.)

It turned out the primitive course was so badly drained that even after the rain had subsided, she and the former Miss Didrikson had to take their shots balanced on boards slogged down to the fairways for them by the grounds crew, and with a gallery of water moccasins following at their heels.

"Still, you can say this much for a cottonmouth anyway, dears. He does help your concentration."

My father had showed up in 1966 at one of her golf clinics.

"What *I* felt when I first saw him was all the recognition between the toaster and the bath."

"You don't think that's taking things a wee bit too far, Jeanie?"

"Afraid I do not, Dee. What I said to him was, All right, now I want you to relax, please, Mr. Buelle. Those shoulders, if you don't mind. And don't you even think about hitting the ball."

"And what I said was: Then just what exactly *am* I supposed to be thinking about, ma'am?"

"You should only be thinking about form, Mr. Buelle."

"But that's all I ever *do* think about—is it?—is it Miss?—Miss *Doogan.*"

My father's drawl, when he wanted it to, could wrap around and disappear into itself, like molasses dripping into molasses. Then again he could harden it with no warning: a ribbon of hot glass plunged into water. In 1966, however, he was still trying to recover from the death of his first wife, and so might have been more painfully drawn-out than usual.

He'd replayed for us how he brushed at the grass with his driver.

"All I wanted to do was come out and play a few balls."

"And I said, I know, Mr. Buelle. I can see that's what you do *want* to do."

"Well, then, it does seem like they'll have to be *thought* about, in the process?"

"Praise be, Mr. Buelle, and let the light shine down on me!"

According to them both, Mama had then dropped down onto the groomed grassy edge of that country club tee box in her crisp, white, paneled skirt; crossed her strong, square, muscular knees; flipped back her dark, blunt-cut hair; settled her long, squared chin at his, and leveled her eyes around his boxlike hips. "And to think, my goodness, I have been wrong all these years, Mr. Buelle. Me and Harvey Penick, the both of us. Well now." And she'd nodded from over her crossed knees, ladylike. "You just go right on ahead there. I'm just going to sit here and try this little trick of thinking about your balls, too."

Of course my father hit the most dribbling shot.

But then afterwards—again this was according to both of them—his bushy red eyebrows had shot up, and he'd pounced, delighted, almost prancing, almost dancing on the pins of his cleats, all while pointing and smiling triumphantly down at his mulligan: "Oh, but aren't you so kind to have left me one more?"

They both wrestle to have the last word.

I turned in under the damp, clenched boards that look like the stomach muscles of the beach house and parked the car on their new, wet raised concrete slab. I hadn't known they'd finally gotten around to putting one down. Against one of the stilts of the house, nailed up crookedly, was their old stenciled sign, crudely warning trespassers off. Half of its lettering now seemed to be missing. I pulled my satchel out of the backseat. The rain had stopped, but the wind rouged up my cheeks and the nape of my neck. I picked through the nets of seaweed blown up against the stair landing; everything looked about the same, the way I remembered, with Mama's trumpet vines crawling up the side of the splintered golf shed, where they kept a few tools and the spare cart.

Now *remember,* chickadees. My father used to wag his finger at us. A big fat house in the city with its nice white columns, and French chandeliers, and a four-car garage, and all that, it's swell, sure, but it really only comes in handy for impressing fool strangers fool enough to be entertained, like babies, like little babies, by mirrors whirling over their heads.

On the upstairs deck I found all the metal storm shutters rolled down, except for the main one over the sliding glass door. I squinted in and banged.

Almost as quickly Mama was there, her nose like a pointer's, her chin long, her cheeks drawn in. She pulled me inside and got my bag off my shoulder before I could react.

"Now isn't it," she let the bag drop and then turned and swished the door closed behind me, "*crusty* out?"

Her way of saying hello: just a quick, light peck in the air next to my cheek; just a reaching up, quickly, gingerly, almost absently, to pat my shoulder with her knobbly red hand. As though she thought she was still overwhelming, and that I was still a gawking four-year-old boy, and she still the Fifty-Foot Woman hauling her trophies into the big house.

It was three months since I'd seen my parents last. But now—and here I had to step back to be sure—Mama seemed to have shrunk. She was slipping down an invisible gangway.

"Cute, Harry!" She pointed at my feet. "Suede loafers. So *sweet* on you."

"What? Thanks, Mama."

"You drive carefully? Did you notice that nasty pothole is still there right after the drawbridge? You take things slowly?"

We have a history of strange accidents in my family. "All in one piece," I held out my hands to show her.

Her gray eyes narrowed at me. She looked as if she wanted to ask me something, leaning forward, on one foot, as if ready to press on the tiller of a question. But then she must have changed her mind. "You know, it could just be your hair is too long, dear, but you look a little *puny* under there."

"Puny" doesn't mean small in her Carolina dialect. "Puny" is her euphemism for peaked.

"Honey, I mean just look at the stick of you! Have you been eating anything at all?"

"Whatever's put in front of me, Mama."

"Well, whatever it is, it's not enough."

She took another look, a minute to fall back a step in those white deck shoes. Then she shook her steel-gray bangs over her eyes, and sighed. She shrugged her shoulders, stiff and cut under that ironed white T-shirt. Her legs were still straight inside those familiar, god-awful beach culottes. But her shins, the veins, they were so pronounced, now—all that blue-green scaffolding as if thrown up for repairs.

No, no, she waved me off, tossing her bulging knuckles in the air, her arthritis was just fine, now that she wasn't playing anymore, now she wasn't paying so much attention to it anymore, it was all in order, although, of course, still a bit of a nuisance, if anything precise needed doing.

"Harry dear, you really do look scrawny. Anything bothering you?"

"No," I lied. "Where's Daddy?"

"Back in the kitchen. Contemplating. Contemplating and constipating, if you want to know. But you won't be able to guess, just now, what he's gone and caught."

"A stingray?"

"Nope."

"A sea turtle?"

"No. It's a sea *bird,* this time. And a big ol' one."

"On live or dead bait?"

She laughed and threw an elbow at me, without touching.

I smiled back, watching her. I had confided to her, once, my theory that Dennis Buelle never could resist the temptation to hook something unwary. That spending his boyhood around here, around all the seine nets tacked up on the fences and the crab traps and hunting guns (he still kept one, upstairs, for safety, in the chest in the corner of their bedroom), he just couldn't help some of his country-boy reflexes. I'd seen him, out in waders waist-deep in a tide smacking over the jetties—this would have been years ago—casting a corked line with a long, gleaming barb on the end of it on which he'd just jabbed a twitching shrimp, dragging the buoy of it over toward a floating gull when nothing else seemed to be biting, curious to see how far a hungry bird might be willing to go.

Mama just waved her hand again. "No, he doesn't go out with tackle anymore. The poor thing blew right here, into our new patio glass. Did you notice?" She pointed at the sliding door, then at the wicker-backed sofa, directing me to sit down. "It happened just a little while ago. We felt a kind of *thunking*." She dropped down next to me, sinking into the faded chintz. "I thought, at first, it was just some of the outdoor furniture, scootching around on the deck, in the wind. Or maybe one of my plant pots rolling around." She adjusted a cushion underneath her. Some sand sprinkled off and to the wide-planked floor. Mama wasn't exactly born a housekeeper. "Anyway, I just went back to making our lunches. I'd peeled all that crawfish yesterday, I told you. And I'd made tartar sauce, but anyway, that's not the point, the point is, what could it *hurt* was what your daddy was saying, I remember, that's exactly what he was saying, what do these doctors know, anyway, what on earth could it really hurt us, a little mayonnaise, right about now? And that's when the poor thing began kicking up against the side of the house. And then it started shrieking."

"Shrieking?"

"All right then, whatever kind of sound a sorely pissed-off Booby makes. That's what your father says it is, although I'm not so sure about species, myself. Anyway! Now that we've had a little rest," she braced both hands beside her thighs and stood, "why don't you come on back, and see for yourself?"

I followed her under the open stairs that lead up to the loft, past the side hallway with their downstairs bath and laundry room, and into the kitchen. My father was sitting hunched on one of the four-legged stools, peering over the serrated edge of a cardboard box.

The box rested on their deeply scarred, butcher-block island. Behind him, the green-tiled counter was apparently triage for blackened pots and dirty dishes. Empty shells had been left to dry on the ledge over the sink. There was a faint smell of hardened salt and fish guts and old crab butter. The brown watermark ringing the room just a few inches under the ceiling had been made by Carla's surge, in 1961.

My father didn't look up, but he did beckon his long finger at me. "Come and see."

What I saw, what registered, with an electric jolt, when I got close enough: that the skin covering my father's hooked finger, and the backs of his bluish hands, it was so shining, so delicate, so translucent, he might have been a man-o'-war washed up on the beach.

"Come *closer,* Harry," he grumbled, irritated. "Don't worry about him trying to escape, or making any sort of fuss. It's not how they got the name, after all."

Under the cloud of his hair the skin on his forehead shimmered, stretched taut over his temples. A few wisps of hair ran down past his long, square jaw. But it was his stomach I couldn't take my eyes from. My father's stomach. It was swollen. His buttoned shirt was dangling over his shorts in a floppy banner.

"Come *on,*" he said impatiently.

I leaned in toward him, just lightly tapping his shoulder; overdone displays were something he mistrusted. I looked past him and down into the open box. Inside, on a folded beach towel, one big, fat, miserable-looking bird squatted.

"So what do you think, son?"

"Nice catch, Daddy."

"Fully grown, too."

Overgrown. Its triangular beak was almost too big for its face. The peacock-colored rings around its eyes gave it a stunned, ghostly look. Its thick brown feathers seemed to drag the weight of its neck too low on its chest, which was a brilliant, startling white.

Then I saw the broken yellow foot jutting to one side, and winced and backed away.

"Sula leucogaster!" my father announced, pleased. "Brown Booby. I checked it in the field book."

"It reminds me more of a white one turned upside down and dunked in it. Poor thing," Mama added.

"You see the foot injury?" He turned to me. "That's our little head-scratcher. We don't know if that happened, just now, when the poor fellow hit the deck, or if that's what hung down and ended up ruddering him off course."

"How'd you manage to get it inside?"

"Jeanie did it. Nothing to it really. Was there, Jeanie?"

"It didn't fight back." Mama peered over the edge of the box. "I just dropped that towel over its poor, dumb head."

"It didn't snap at you, Mama?"

"Didn't I just *finish,*" Daddy stiffened, and shot his bushy white eyebrows up, "explaining to you they are extremely *passive* creatures?"

I was too busy listening to his breathing. Every intake a slight effort. More audible than it should have been. Not a gasp. Not a pant. Not a wheeze. My father wasn't straining. It was only the sound of ropes being pulled, giving the stagehands away.

"Dee," Mama sighed. "I don't see why you're so certain it is a Booby." She tried sorting through some of the dirty dishes on the counter. "They don't come on land, as I recall."

He aimed his stomach at her like a cannonball. "Now, what are you talking about? Of *course* they come on land! All birds have to, at some point. It's just as I said, this one's been blown out of his way in some accident or other, and since we're the farthest house out, at this end, he probably made for us, thinking we might be a harbor of some kind. A kind of rookery. A safe haven."

At that I looked down doubtfully.

"*He,* Daddy?" I wiped my neck. October, and they could have been using the air-conditioning, but weren't.

"I was speaking, son, as should have been *perfectly* obvious, in the generic."

"Now that bird's anything but," Mama said.

My father threw his hands up. "I meant, in the sense of a *general rule.*"

What is the general rule, in the Buelle household?

None of us have any trouble acting irritated. Exasperated. Dismayed. Offended. Annoyed. We like to be smart-asses, and occasionally can get foulmouthed—if the occasion demands. We banter, frown, goad, tease, complain, joke, and scold one another.

But the general rule, underneath it all, through thick and thin, through *Sturm und Drang,* is never to get upset. The main thing is always to stay in control. Even in the middle of what might be, of what any other person might be reasonable to think of as, an actual drama.

My sister knows better than any of us how to be casual. How to get up quickly after a fall. How to recover, and stick her chin out, and shrug, and get on with whatever it was that needed overcoming. Because what was self-consciousness, after all, chickadees, but poor reflexes? What was embarrassment, except a bone imperfectly swallowed?

My father was trying to get the Booby's attention by snapping his soft fingers. It didn't seem to notice.

"I know!" I brightened, feeling suddenly relieved for it. "I can get back in the car and take it over to the wildlife refuge."

"No, dear, we've already gone over that." Mama popped a cold shrimp into her mouth and reached up to put a platter away in one of the open cabinets. "Turns out, they've changed their schedule out there. They shut down by three o'clock now, on Fridays."

I hovered near the box, my hands fluttering protectively over it. "Well, there must be some other kind of service or drop-off, somewhere? Things do need to be rescued, even on Fridays."

"I think this is a good setup." My father stared down into the cardboard box as though into a sterile petri dish. "I think we can manage it, for the time being."

Mama directed me toward the other stool and changed the subject. "Come on, you just got here, and I haven't even asked you—do you want something to eat? A crawfish appetizer, now how about that? Or some shrimp? Or would you rather just wait for Sarah and dinner?"

"I'll wait," I gave in and sat down.

My father pulled his glasses up from the chain at the top of his stomach, and looking through them, stared hard across the battered island at me.

"So now, son. How are you?"

· 3 ·

I stared, casually, back at him.

But I was wondering: What are you seeing, Daddy? What can you make out of me, from behind those gray, watery eyes? Is that a pale Village poof you see, one who makes you cringe a little, in his tight black jeans, and with his curly black hair so like his dead mother's—but with more height than you, and with your dragging scoop of a jaw? Did you notice my skin the way I noticed yours—register how thick or how thin it was? How well can you make out the bubble of me, Daddy, from inside your own filmy bubble? How loud, how loud the beating is inside here, Daddy, and how loud it must be, inside yours. But how muffled we all were, anywhere outside ourselves. How completely soundproofed every human being is from every other one, after all.

"Fine, Dad."

"You sure?"

"You?"

"Oh I've been doing some great thinking out here. Mulling over some really exceptional things."

"Sounds promising."

"You won't even guess the half of it. And I've been getting a little exercise, too. Did you know? It's never too late to be sure of yourself. You should see me on all the stairs. Nothing to it. Those beta-blockers, I knew it, they were all to blame for slowing me down." He dropped his chin toward his neck, as if to let some air pass. "Plus, Jeanie and I've decided we're going to take a few more drives around the beach, this time out. Aren't we, Jeanie? Show off a bit to the mullet. I'm getting so stout. Look at that! Orotund. I'm practically at full Sumo strength."

I blinked at Mama, who was smiling serenely and swabbing a plate with a napkin.

"He thinks he's *cute,*" she warned.

Outside the surf was pounding steadily, like an army over an army.

"Of course," my father sighed and raised a bushy eyebrow, "you have to understand, it's nothing new for me. Being a *darling.*"

And here is the thing about fame, about being one of the theater's most prominent, white-haired Southern icons: you don't get to hold on to that without knowing, wily, instinctive, how to be disarming.

Sarah and I, on the other hand, are natural-born social dweebs. We were homeschooled in the beginning, partly because of her epilepsy, but partly because my parents hoped we might be less awkward, less tongue-tied, if we had more time to adjust to breathing a celebrity's oxygen.

We were kept away from my father's performances, safe from the glare of his openings and the excitement of his awards, because it did seem a little unjust, we overheard him explain, to make children bear the weight of expectation too early. When the season was over and he was at home again we were sometimes dragged downstairs in the big house to try our manners out on his friends and colleagues, or on the interviewers who came to Texas to talk about his long winning streak, taking notes under the mirrored chandeliers.

For the most part Sarah and I stayed in our bedrooms, hiding out until we were allowed to start prep school. To be fair, by the time I was twelve I had read all of Chekhov and half of Shakespeare, and my sister had mastered the concert violin.

Mama turned and held her knuckles up toward all the bugs trapped in the well of the kitchen light.

"I just wish my puffy joints were a little more *darling.*"

"But they *are,* Jeanie-pie!" my father said quickly, although without moving on his stool to touch her. It's another, unspoken Buelle rule: physical attraction is a private affair.

"Anyhow." She shrugged and let her knuckles fall to her side, and then smiled so all her even white teeth showed. And there it was: some things about her would always be indestructible. "What's there left to gripe about, at this point, really? Growing old is all gravy."

"And all the same color," he shot back.

"Growing old is a dog left to chew his bone."

"Only we be the bone."

Willie and Able were awfully quiet. Usually being at the beach house, the pounding of the waves, drove them into hysterics. "Where are the pups?"

"Upstairs." My father reached for the butcher block and swiveled back around on his stool. "Locked up in our bedroom, because our unexpected guest here is so *fanthy.*"

He actually did it. Glanced at me and let the word come out with that light, mocking lisp. He snapped his long fingers twice, suddenly sharp.

The bird reacted, stretching its head on its long neck as though it were finally awake and trying to pull itself out of a sleeve.

"Daddy, you want me to *scootchy* on up and let them out?"

"What's that?" he blinked.

"I mean, this box is so perfect. It's big enough to keep the doggies out, I'm sure. I'm *sure* it would be safe. And wouldn't a little company be all right with you, *sweetie,* you funny little old *thang?*" I waved one hand over the bird and fixed the other on my hip and turned my voice up all precious and soft and cooing. "Wouldn't that be all right with you, *honey,* if we let those feisty little meanies out?"

I felt him wince. But when I turned, the wrinkles had all fallen back into their troops around his eyes.

"Jeanie, I'm just going to say this right out. I don't know *why* this sort of thing is about all the parental instinct I ever see out of my children." He frowned at her, scratching his flaking scalp. "Would someone please explain it to me? One year to the end of the millennium, to the end of an era, for all we know, and look, they stand at zilch for progeny. Why is that?"

"Absence of prayer, dear?"

"Enough." I threw up my hands and cut them short.

This was exactly why Sarah and I had bought those terriers, all those years ago: to put an end to all the reproductive whining. As if the answer to any family's problems was always—why not?—to mix in more family. As if either one of us would ever give in to our parents' wild, imaginative hopes for bouncing baby bundles. It's not our fault, Sarah once nudged me and jerked her chin toward them, certain old dogs can't perform certain complicated tricks. Mother Nature has her limits.

I tossed my head toward the upstairs. "I guess I'm going up and unpacking. See you in a little bit."

"Son. Harry. Wait. Wait? Would you please?"

It was the pleading tone. It was my father's hands. I did a double take. They were fluttering, delicately. They were twitching, blue in the air now, floating, flitting, searching at the square hollow of his throat. He tried steadying them on his loose collar, but they kept getting away from him, like untied flies. "Harry? Son? Couldn't you—please. Would you wait, for just one minute, to, to come and help me—"

His gray lips were trembling. I was so amazed, I couldn't move.

"Oh, for *God's* sake!" he swore when I stayed frozen. "Won't *somebody* in this room carry this Booby into my study for me, first?"

"All right, Dee. Calm down."

In one movement Mama lifted the cardboard box off the

butcher block, catching it crookedly on one knee when it fell to her side, the bird flapping awkwardly over the edge of it.

"Mama, wait, I—"

"Harry, dear, you just stay where you are, it's all right, go on up, like you said, and let the boys out for us. I've got this under control." She adjusted her grip on the box and tossed her hair out of her eyes. "Now *why* in your study, Dee?"

He looked down surprised at her. "Because I thought I might read to him!"

"Oh, for heaven's sake."

"Well, you probably can't tell what a Booby needs, by looking."

"Go on, then."

He nodded at her and pushed away from the island.

I watched him ease his weight off the stool. How he slipped from it, laboriously, as though he were sliding through a gum. When he was finally on his feet, he straightened his long back, slowly, repositioning the balloon of his stomach in front of him, his white cotton shirt still waving in that drooping flag over his shorts; and then he followed her out of the room, eyes fixed on her back, concentrated, staring hard at some point that went through the middle of her shoulder blades. And I felt something heave in my stomach. Was this really my father, having to focus on something as simple as what he wanted to do next?

· 4 ·

No keening. No wailing. No howling. All that happened when I opened up the bedroom door was that Willie and Able shot out between my legs, scraping them and making a beeline for the stairs.

Before closing the door again I looked in and saw one of my father's old sweaters, draped over the back of the Windsor rocker, and another one folded in the corner on top of the brass-plated chest, where they hid the gun, and kept extra blankets, and where Mama stored a pair of old cleats and a few boxes of chipped Titleists, for days when she still felt like shooting balls into the Gulf. I had to duck as I closed the door; everything up here still low and makeshift, unrefurbished. But they preferred it that way.

Now here, you see here, my father would tell one of the rare, fortunate visitors (one of his producers or financial backers) invited up into this inner sanctum: here, you see it, over on this side of the floor, underneath this window, this is where I remember, and I remember it with perfect clarity, where I had a little trundle bed I was allowed to sleep in if the weather was cool enough. There were no walls up here, during the Depression, only the whole upper floor open, it was an attic, and for the most part of course we all had to sleep downstairs, where we could catch a breeze. But on some nights, I used to lie here and read for as long as I could, a few, tattered, hairy-spined books—Lord knows how on earth we got them, they must have come down from better times, my parents had lived in town, and my father had been a clerk—but the point is, by whatever light I could get my hands on I stayed up and read, sometimes kerosene, sometimes only a sliver of yellow moon. Crying for Queequeg, and Sir Thomas More. Oh, many, many was the night when I drifted off, like that, with the sound of the June bugs slamming against the windows, and the sawing of the waves, and dreamed of getting away, as fast as I could, far, far away, to some foreign place, away from the damp and the sump of it all—away out West. Oh, you had to dream, chickadees! He would suddenly turn to us, remembering we were there, practicing our manners on his guest. You had to imagine bravely! To show no fear. You had to believe the world would one day split like a peach for you, like a book at its spine, like a grub when you squeezed it between your fingers. You had to believe, in the end, the world had as much guts as you did.

He'd bought the long-lost family beach house back, when he

finally could, when he finally had the money to (it was about the time he married Helen, our mother, and was pulling in extra profits from the movie versions of his plays); and then, whenever anyone asked why on earth he had wanted to hang on to a tumble-down box on stilts, he had given it out, confident, that no one should ever be ashamed of where he came from—and besides, there was something to be said for owning the only house on this strip of beach to survive Hurricane Carla.

"But Dad," I'd groaned, putting my summer reading down on my sweating lap. This would have been about the time I was a sophomore in college; the book came from an ecology course I was taking because basic biology was too much for me. "You don't really believe that, do you? You don't think we'll get the same kind of protection, can count on the same kind of coastal conditions, anymore? We can't expect to have the same luck as the people who owned this place back in '61. The experts, all the scientists, they *know* now—there's just been way too much erosion out here."

My father lifted his chin up over the pages of his *Southern Review,* and looked across the wooden deck rail, out over the lumpen dunes, through the salt haze toward a new, distant oil platform. He'd frowned over his peeling nose. Oil might get some of his plays funding, but that didn't mean he had to approve of it. There is absolutely nothing more wasteful, he was fond of complaining, than having to burn your own fat to make a light.

"Go on, son?"

"All I'm saying is, compared to what there probably was out here, at one time, there's hardly any beach left around this place to speak of at all now. Certainly nothing like what La Salle's crew saw. Basically all we're doing is balancing on the lip of a bucket." I remember being happy with that turn of phrase, lifting myself up on my hands, letting the textbook slide down between my burned legs. "See, there? Maybe that shelf will build up again, someday—who knows? But you don't depend on something like a sandbar. What came around once doesn't necessarily come around again." My chest and stomach felt long and gleaming in the sun; I'd stretched them out, gorgeous.

My father stared at where the waves were plainly tearing at us with their white teeth.

"Oh my *God!*" He threw his review down and grabbed fistfuls of his graying hair in mock horror. "You mean to tell me, all of life is *transient?*"

"Daddy . . ."

He shook his head slowly and sighed and settled comfortably back down into his lounge chair. "You know, I don't know what you think you're accomplishing by speaking to your father in that kind of *demoralizing* way." He had smiled and closed his eyes and swung his white feet over the edge of the cushion. "I don't know why I'm even bothering to send you and Sarah to college at all, if all it's going to do is turn you into a couple of rank and unpleasant pessimists."

"But I'm not a pessimist, Daddy. I'm a— I'm—" I hesitated. "I'm practical."

"And I'm not?"

"I thought college was the cat's meow, myself," Jean said from her own chair, pulling her dark sunglasses down and resting them on the end of her pointed nose, dropping her chin over the neckline of her large, concealing one-piece swimsuit. "I loved all the girls and all the competition."

But my father shook his head and reached down for his magazine. He didn't have to say it. I knew that in his opinion a university degree was something necessary only for the unproven, the obscure—like a driver's license carried by a tourist in a foreign country. While talent, if possessed, would always be recognized at a great distance.

What was left of my old beach bedroom looked like an abandoned monk's cell. The wicker bookcase—I'd picked out its dainty lines myself—was still in one piece, in the corner, but now unspooling curls of rattan bandaging. The high window was thick with sand scratches and bug splatterings. My sailboat curtains were gone, for some reason. I turned and looked inside the narrow closet and found a three-year-old pair of cracked flip-flops, from the last time we'd all managed to meet out here, and a row of new pink plastic hangers Mama must have just supplied. Before we got too old, Sarah and I used to hang from these clothes rods, swinging and talking to each other through the thin, makeshift walls.

Sometimes I would hear her muttering to herself, arguing, or singing, but there was always a catch: if I heard nothing at all coming from her side for too long, then it was my responsibility (and I knew this because I'd had it hammered into me a thousand times) to go over and check up on her.

"Get out of here, Harry."

Her mattress was always put directly on the floor, as a precaution. That day, her sheet music had been fanned out in front of her scaly, twelve-year-old knees.

"I'm just visiting, Sar."

"You are penetrating my peripheral vision."

Her cheeks as usual were puffy. Some of the medications caused swelling. She slid the papers to one side, and stared casually up at my pitted and pimpled face. I looked quickly away. Distortions in the visual field can cause problems for epileptics.

"What have you been doing, Harry?"

"I just wanted to see if you were all right."

"So what does it look like?" She reached for a pencil. She'd given up the violin by then and was telling everyone she was going to be a great composer, which was why she didn't like coming out to the beach—it distorted her internal rhythms. Besides, the sun turned her hair red.

"I so completely hate it here," I sighed and leaned inside her doorway and folded my arms.

The everlasting roll of the waves. The feeling of being pinned down by something large and heavy. Summer heat so intense the Gulf ran as hot as a bath. Our window air conditioners could only be turned on at night because Freon, Jean said, was unhealthy.

"I'm going stir-crazy, Sar. I think," I said casually, "I'll go for a walk behind the dunes when it gets cooler."

"You'll get all the bone flies," she nodded doubtfully.

"I'll repel them with my sheer disgust." I scraped one of my flip-flops over the floor, but kept watching her for signs. "You sure you're not feeling any way puny?"

She gave me a steady look. "I know why it is you don't have any girlfriends, Har. It's because you're so skinny and white, if you took off all your clothes, you'd look like a pile of sticks with glue running down them."

And here is the thing about Sarah. You have to be careful around her.

Not just because the doctors and psychologists recommend it. Not necessarily just because stress is known in some cases to make an epileptic's condition worse, bumping up the number of her bad versus good days, sometimes altering the effects of otherwise trustworthy medication; not because you might compromise the mood of the patient toward her prognosis; but because you never could be certain whether or not Sarah Buelle was going to let you in, allow you to get close enough to admit that you might actually be thinking about her, trying to imagine her feelings, her world, her dreams, her fears, her thoughts—or whether, instead, your smallest gesture of concern would drive her down into that deep, cold place where she lay perfectly still, perfectly steady, and perfectly sensible, green eyes looking up at you, that mattress suddenly plunged to the bottom of a lake: and her mouth ready to launch the first casual missile that popped into it.

Outside my square of window the sky was cream colored, the flat look of malt in a glass. I wrinkled my nose and beat the dust off my limp pillows. Jean may have learned how to cook and garden, but again, she wasn't a natural housewife.

All of a sudden she was behind me.

"My curtains, Ma?"

"I know, dear." She shook her head sadly and came in. "It's just, you see, they got so plain *pitiful* I finally had to pull them down. Poor little old sailboats."

"I thought you two liked this place looking all ragged and relaxed."

"There are limits, dear."

"Some things you just don't like to see falling to pieces?"

"That must be it."

She smiled and nodded and folded her arms and leaned against the thin wall, watching me while I put my T-shirts away. From the corner of my eye I saw the skin pooling slackly above her collarbone. She was so much looser, now that she was old.

"Harry, dear? I'm so glad you're here."

"I come when I'm called, Mama."

"Are you sure you didn't have to leave anything overly pressing?"

"I've been having a little trouble with the next act of my new play."

She squinted at me the way she had earlier, and hesitated—though not for long. Mama was never one to get stuck in a bunker. She twisted her shoulders free from the wall.

"Well, dear, sometimes it's good to put things aside for a while, isn't it?"

"Did you come up for something?"

"Oh. Well now."

"It's all right. Go on, say it."

"Nothing, really. I was just wondering how you thought your father looked?"

The trick, she once explained to me, many years ago, leaning over my quivering, eight-year-old body, her feet planted behind mine in the dense turf, her breath brushing the top of my head, hands squeezing my arms, the trick, Harry dear, is always to understand exactly how much *effort* something should take. Now, there will always be moments, of course, when you'll have to be very aggressive. But then again, there are times when, if we allow whatever it is that we want to *overwork* us, we'll do nothing but burn up our two legs right under our hips. The trick is to feel the right amount of force, the very center of the stroke, which is like a weight hanging down from the middle of your chin—like this. And here's the important thing, dear, the most important thing of all: never, *never* put yourself in a position where you're only thinking about the *hole.* Never put yourself in a place where the hole actually becomes something bigger than you are. Do you understand me? Good. Now. Head down, and back straight. Clubhead square at address.

"I think he looks lousy." I kept my head down.

"Those beta-blockers were so awful, though."

"But all that extra weight, Mama—he looks like he just came out of the Sudan."

She seemed to be holding back again. Then she raised her eyes level, and with perfect distance, into mine.

"That's not really it, dear," she shook her head, matter-of-fact. "It has nothing to do with how much or how little your daddy's been eating. It's just one of the side effects of this kind of condition. The heart, being a pump and all, when it slows down, it's naturally going to have a harder time pushing fluids out of the—"

I cut her off, holding my hands up. "Right, right, I got it. I only meant— I don't need to— I'm just saying he looks—"

The bedroom seemed to ring, the way every room in a beach house does. I was left hanging, reaching for the right word. The load-bearing word. The word that, when you first begin studying plays, when you first begin dreaming of people moving around, marching around, in the order they've been told to—the word you learn is really an action in disguise.

"Uncomfortable." No, that wasn't it. I looked down into the drawer. "Even . . . well . . . precarious. Shouldn't we be thinking about staying closer in to the hospital?"

She bent and tugged at the faded fringe on my bedspread, taking a shot at straightening the sheets. "Harry, dear, no offense, you know, but there's not a chance in Hillje or Harrisburg I'm going to let them put another one of those catheters up his you-know-what, and have people poking in at him every two hours. Do you want to know something about precarious? Well, all right, then I'll tell you. Your father told me that, the last time, when we had to spend so much time up in the cardiac unit, he felt crazy enough to kill all the night nurses, go out and gouge them in the necks with his IV. And he nearly meant that, Harry. He said he felt like a lump of C-4 ready to go off."

"But—but you never—!"

"Well no, dear, why would I?" she blinked. "There was no point getting you and Sarah all bent out of shape for no reason. It was just those drugs. That's what I'm telling you. That's what you need to see. He might be getting a shade heavy without them, but he can also think so much more clearly."

I had to finish putting my socks away. If I didn't, if she saw me quick to believe my father was brute enough to massacre a floor full of nurses, she would think I was a drama queen.

"Stop looking at me that way, Mama. I understand."

"*Was* I looking, dear?"

"It's funny, I thought Sarah and Paul would be here by now."

"I guess they will be, soon enough." She gave the hem of the spread one last jerk. "So the only thing we *really* have to worry about now, I suppose, is whether or not your daddy is going to want to throw poor Paul off the sundeck. I keep reminding him he's just a boy; he can't help being as excitable as he is. There's just no call to get all bent out of shape over a silly boy."

I went on rearranging my underwear. I had to. If I didn't, she would see the corners of my eyes, suddenly leaking.

"Anyhow, you know how those two are always so late. That Paul, he's such a mess, isn't he? But I know he cares for our Sarah, so of course everything's going to be all right, in the end. And now that Dee's more himself again, I think he'll be more patient. Did you notice, back on the Fourth, at the big house, how hard he and Paul were trying around each other?"

"Mama?"

"You haven't even told me if you're seeing anyone seriously right now." She suddenly brushed her hand over my shoulder, smiling.

"Mama?"

"You could have brought someone down, you know. I'm sure we would have liked meeting one of your friends. That nice boy I spoke to on the phone a few weeks ago. He sounded so sweet."

"Mama." Was it deliberate, or was her hearing going along with the skin at her neck? *"Jeanie!"* I finally echoed my father downstairs.

"What, dear?"

"It's Daddy. He's been calling your name and swearing."

· 5 ·

The unpainted French doors leading out to my father's study—an old side porch he'd had enclosed years ago, so he could get some peace and privacy (this meant get away from us all, even at the beach)—were thrown back. Willie and Able were barking just inside the musty room, wriggling and panting and crouching down on their haunches, all their weight dumped into their raggy gray rumps, like sandbags.

Mama glided past me and folded her arms, looking down at them.

"Well? What is it?"

"It took you long enough to get down here," my father complained.

"Is this an emergency?"

"It's *shit!*" he announced.

He was blinking at us, sitting back inside the slatted arms of his rolling chair. Underneath the pitched roof, surrounded by the sharp corners of his bookshelves and silhouetted against all those scratched, square-paned windows, he looked soft and blurred.

Mama sighed. "Hush now, Willie."

"It's *shit,*" he repeated, but this time in a more hurt tone, and pointed to the wilting cardboard at his feet.

"Oh now," Mama laughed.

He winced. "I don't see there's anything to be so *hilarious* about. That towel, the way we lined the box, it was a bad idea. I'd just like to know who thought of it. We should have used plastic, or newspaper, or butcher paper or, or—" His hands were fluttering again, uncontrollably, this time in the direction of the journals and reviews piled at his feet.

I was quick this time. "Magazines, Daddy."

"That's right! That's what we should have used."

I leaned over and in to see the Booby still balancing to one side of its broken foot. Only now it seemed to be leaning away from all the noise and commotion. Or maybe it was disgusted by the blue-green pool that had eddied out and was soaking under its feet.

I pulled away but heard my voice say, surprisingly, "I'll clean it up."

"Don't be silly." Mama waved me off. "I'll do it."

"Mama?"

"Dear. Move your tushie."

"Mama."

"I mean it, now."

"Oh for God's sake," my father started from his chair. "Let's not be so *genteel* about this. I guess *I'll* have to do it. Since it's obvious neither one of you has ever changed a diaper."

"Both of you boys, stop your fussing." She elbowed past me. "Harry, pull Willie and Able back. And Dee, keep still."

We did as we were told. After I'd calmed the dogs with one of their punctured rubber chew toys, she grabbed the bird's box by one corner and slid it away from his desk.

My father rolled off to one side in his chair, tucking his chin in. When she stopped at the edge of the room, he opened his mouth and closed it and then opened it again.

"I'm so sorry, Jeanie."

"What for, dear?"

"You know for what. I shouldn't have snapped at you that way. Not—not *now*." He tossed his hand in my direction—whether this was to include me in his explanation, or banish me, or blame me, I couldn't tell.

"Oh, well. We'll just have to hope Harry can get over it." She folded down next to the box, cross-legged, wincing and reaching up to cover her mouth and a cough. "I think he's used to seeing us tussle—aren't you, dear? You can take what we dish out around here, can't you?"

My father swiveled suddenly toward me. Eyes steady, studying me. Almost hopeful. Then just as quickly he turned away.

"Jeanie? Jeanie? What time is it? How late is it now? I wonder why Sarah hasn't called us yet."

"You know she doesn't call from the road. She doesn't like the waves or the signals or the cell phone batteries or what have you, near her head. Be easy, I'm sure they're almost here."

"Well *Paul* could use the damn thing, couldn't he?"

She didn't seem to hear this. She was reaching in to stroke the bird's gleaming brown head.

"They'll be pulling in any minute I'm sure, Daddy."

"But you would think someone as hyperactive as Paul would cover ground faster! I don't see," he ran his fingers through his tangled hair, "how we could all stand there and let her marry such a toddler. He's not just too young for her; he's too young for all of us. Jeanie. Jeanie! Do you know what?"

"Yes, Dee?" she sighed, impatient. She was trying to pull the towel out from under the bird, a magician trying not to disturb the table china.

"What is it, Daddy?" I stepped in.

"We ought to give him a bath! Just like the dogs!"

His face was alight now. All that concern, all that paying attention to details—over nothing but a bird.

"You mean Paul?" I said coolly.

"What? What?"

"Oh, I don't think it's necessary, Dad. You know they discovered bathing in Eastern Europe a long while back. It was a big hit with the Romans and all."

I saw him grow more and more confused.

"What? What are you saying to me?"

His round eyes were bewildered. "Jeanie? Jeanie?" He turned away. "Look. Just look at that! You only have to watch the poor thing. He really needs something extra, he's so miserable, he's just not used to this sort of, of . . . dishevelment. He's used to shitting on the fly. My Jeanie-pie?"

"*What,* Dee?"

"What do you think of my little bathing idea?"

She squeezed her eyes shut and then opened them. "Fine, dear, fine. But not in the kitchen, please. I'm trying to keep it tidy in there. You can use the downstairs bath."

"My *dream* of Jeanie!"

"You better not even think about it. You can do it yourself. You'll want to make sure everything's done the right way this time, won't you?"

"That's true." He turned to me and nodded, excited.

I looked into his flushed, contorted face. "Dad—Daddy?"

"Okay now, son, listen, here's the plan. You pick him up and take him over there. You *can* bring yourself to carry him this time? Yes? Not so *thqueamish,* this time? Oh dear. Now what's this I see? Is that doubt, is that refusal written all over my son's brow?"

So there was no point worrying about him going soft. "It's objection, Daddy," I said casually. "On grounds of logic."

"But what could be more logical than setting a bird in a tub of water?"

I pointed out the windows.

"Oh, but Harry, now, listen, you're being too *literal* you know, son. That's such a mistake. I've told you that before. I've *warned* you. You have to understand, only small minds take refuge in the obvious. Only *small* minds see the forest where there are trees. Remember that now, my boy, my boy. Now, be your father's sensible son, would you? And help me get this Booby into the bathroom."

· 6 ·

It would have been nice if my grandparents hadn't been killed in a freak fishing-pier accident. Who knows, we might have ended up a simple, anonymous family.

Jeanie did her best with what she found when she moved into the big house with us in 1967. She explained to us why she'd let our slow-moving nanny go: I'm used to working with all *sorts* of people on my own, dears, amateurs and professionals. . . . It's all right, she said, rubbing her hands together over us. I think we can manage it between us.

Among the things she taught us, sitting cross-legged on the rug, and tossing back her short, strangely rough hair:

In the bathtub, the best way to soap yourself was all around in a figure eight. (She demonstrated this by rubbing a dry bar of soap all over her rippling muscles, without taking her clothes off.)

Over the sink she said: brush your teeth hard enough to make them squeak, dears, but not so hard you bloody your gums. A toothbrush, chickadees, is not a hacksaw.

We were taught to pick our clothes out of our closets as if at any moment we might be flushed out for a junior mission to the United Nations. We learned that shoes should always be comfortable enough to sprint in. When the new medications finally calmed Sarah's seizures, and we'd outgrown our parade of college-girl tutors, Jean got us ready for prep school, advising us to walk into our new classrooms and immediately sit down and look beadily into our teachers' eyes, to show we were interested in their subjects. This won you brownie points, along with remembering the four cardinal laws of the physical universe: Eyes are attached to ears. Noses are attached to mouths. Hands are attached to your brain. Feet, never mind appearances, are what keep the ground underneath you.

The most important rule of all, however, was one of good sportsmanship. Always, always be fair, my chickadees. Remember that while the world still tilts more to one side than the other, we have to do our best to compensate. (Because Sarah wasn't allowed to ride a bicycle, for Christmas her present was a hi-fi stereo. Because she got the first stereo, the next year I got the first eight-track tape recorder. Because I had the eight-track, she got the Angora rabbit. And so on, and so on, minutely superintended by Jean. The general idea being that everything should come out evenly, in the end; everything, in the big scheme of things, should be reasonable to all involved.)

Sarah was the first one of us to call her Mama. We were still as small as cubs beside her when she brought us out to the beach and kept us busy while our father worked, taking us over the boardwalk through the dunes, gripping our hands so the wind wouldn't knock us back—guiding us in until Sarah bobbed inside the inflated muscles of her life jacket. On some days the Gulf was so clear and warm the water circled us in a huge green disk. On others it was brown, heavy with sand, the waves snapping down like turtles' beaks.

One day Sarah said, "Mama, this water is unacceptable."

When my father was ready to leave on one of his trips, he told us to mind whatever our Jeanie told us, and to stop crying, for goodness' sake, we were intelligent children, *his* children, and could be expected to understand the essential restlessness of the artistic spirit.

"Trust me, my chickadees," he used her word. "Separations are good for us. They make us stronger."

When he came back from Los Angeles or Boston or New York or Dallas, we would run up to him in the foyer of the big house and circle him with eager questions:

How many people had there been this time?

Did they stand up when they clapped? For how long?

Did *you* clap, Daddy? Why? Didn't that seem, you know, conceited?

And what did the newspapers say afterwards?

"Oh, my chickadees, my chickadees!" He would laugh, proudly, and hold his arms out as if he wanted to hug something just over our heads. "This one, I tell you, it was like taking candy from a baby. It was like shooting fish in a barrel. It was like falling backwards into a bowl of oatmeal. Now who would have ever *thunk* they'd go on and on, like this, about some little ol' scallawag out of the backwaters?"

My father, quite simply, never experienced a lull in his career. The plays kept on pouring out of him. Night after night. Year after year. Award after award. As though he understood, better than anyone else did, what people wanted to hear when a room went dark. As though he knew what they wanted most was to be loved, and held, and catered to; and then scolded, and cheated, and fooled, and cosseted, and betrayed, and then, and then, at the very last possible moment, when it was almost too late, when they could hardly stand it anymore, handed something so perfect, something so beautiful, so polished, so pure, it made up for the long beating they'd just taken. And yet still they went through the lobby and breathed deeply, more easily, the minute they were safely out and away from it.

"He seems happy enough," Daddy said from his seat on the toilet lid.

The bird wasn't complaining. Its broken foot was hanging uselessly down, the other one kicking with a smooth, swanlike motion. Either because of the oval shape of the tub or because it could only paddle on one side, it went in a circle, and only in one direction, calmly.

Mama had just taken another wet towel out of the bathroom to the laundry, shaking her head at us.

I said, leaning against the pedestal sink, keeping away from the overflow, "Staying afloat is happy, I guess."

"Well, but animals, you know." He tugged on one of his long earlobes. "They don't really know what they're in for, do they?"

Everything was quiet except for the bird's sloshing.

"Did I tell you?" he looked up abruptly. "I've started to get a few things down on paper again."

"You already told me, Dad. Are you sure you should be?"

"What?"

"Working now."

He massaged one of his knees, looking around the room as if it were suddenly beneath him. But then during the Depression, as he liked to remind us, there'd been no indoor plumbing in the house at all. "You think I'd be better off just sitting here?"

"Well not *here.*"

"Shows how much you know about the difference. Retirement, son, is composting. It's rot. Trust me. And listen to that. Just listen. Do you hear it? You hear? Nothing. It's never a good idea to step too far out of things. The phone will stop ringing on you."

This part was, truly, rot. They rarely gave out their number here; only to their closest friends. This was their retreat, their private refuge. "You're supposed to be relaxing, Dad."

"Maybe you've been relaxing enough for the both of us. I notice you haven't had anything produced lately." He looked uncertainly at me. "You're not working, I hope, on another one of those impenetrable, experimental things? People standing around half-naked with their hands up, waiting for random stage directions to float down from the ceiling? Please, Harry? Not more of that?"

The critics had been resounding on that one, sending their squawks and honks migrating, in a chorus, south toward my father. "I liked it, Dad."

"Harry, are you ever going to try and write something that might actually get you a foothold?"

"I'm sure I'll hit one out of the park one of these days."

"But it doesn't seem like you even *want* to. I don't understand it. And I've put you in touch with so many of the right people." He leaned forward and made a brisk show of pushing the water toward the Booby with the back of his transparent hand. As if that were necessary. As if an element wouldn't balance properly on its own.

"I don't understand," he repeated, and he wrung out his fingers. "It's fairly simple, Harry. Work has to have authority. It has to have currency. It has to have sweep. If it doesn't have these things, no one will give you the time of day for it. Just take a look at what's on the stage right now. It's all the usual, broad stuff. War and God and mathematics and sex and epic . . . epidemics." On the last word, he winced.

"Worrying about something, Daddy?"

"No. I am *not* worried. I could still go *mano a mano* with any of those young Turks any time of day, if I wanted to!" He bristled. "All I'm saying is, you have to put your ear to the ground, son, and know what you're after. You have to pound out something plain, something that people can *understand,* that can be heard all the way to China, if it has to. It's that easy. And I tell you what else, son. You need to take care of yourself, for the length of the journey. It's a long one. Look at you. What are you now? A waif? Is it the latest trend? I see you've been biting your nails again."

"And?"

"Well, you'd just better not let Jeanie catch you at it. She'll give you her the-body-is-an-island lecture." He dropped his chin down on his neck, staring down at his bloated stomach, which rested in turn on his thighs. From my angle, my father's body looked like a series of ledges, or drop-offs. "Of course, the body's also just pure dross." He shrugged. "A nuisance. Like an alarm clock that won't stop."

I bent forward quickly and reached for the spigot to get some fresh water going into the tub. I relaxed when it came out in its roar. "So how long," I said over it, "are you planning on staying out here?" The Booby was hurrying away from the gush, its foot scraping bottom.

"I don't know. Would you turn that off now? We're still discussing it. How long will you go on staying up there? I've told you before. There's no reason to be in the city all the time. The man makes Broadway come to him. Sarah, now, she's only a few hours away from us, by car."

"Then I wonder why it's taking her so long to get here."

"We have to make allowances for her."

"I do, Daddy."

"Do you know"—he brightened—"I've just remembered I used to give you both baths, in this tub!"

I looked closely at the green tiles. But nothing sprang back with the bounce of memory.

"You don't remember it? Oh, but you should have seen yourself, back then you were such a beanpole, son, even then. You take so much after your mother's side of the family, in the way of frame,

I mean. She was so delicate. It must have been, yes, yes, that's right, it was just after she died. When the three of us were still alone in the world." He opened his mouth as if to go on, but then stopped, as if surprised, as if he'd come around a corner to find a suitcase left loaded with explosives. "You really don't remember?"

"Sorry, Daddy."

"I just finished explaining, though. It's because you were so *frail.*"

Mama put her head in around the corner.

"You know, boys, I do hate to interrupt all these deluxe personalized spa services, but Harry, dear, would you come out here and talk to Paul on the phone for me? I've just started in on boning the fish, and *now* they call, and it turns out they've stopped in their car somewhere to watch the weather or some such thing, and I don't know why he wants to tell us all about it right this minute but he's getting all descriptive and excited and Slavic about it and I *know* I should show more patience, but I must be saving it all for later. You don't mind, do you dear?"

I shook my head and pushed my tailbone away from the sink.

"And what's with *you?*" she pointed the boning knife at my father.

He held his hands up. "Don't shoot! The hydrotherapy."

"Looks to me more like some confused old man babysitting a scavenger."

"Well it looks to me like some dotty old woman got the weaponry out too soon."

No reason to think Timothy was going to call. I hadn't given him the number here. I didn't want to hear from him. What was there left to say? He'd turned out more or less like all the rest. A charade. Barricading himself behind the bedroom door, melodramatically. Then the stalling, the shuffling out, apologetic, embarrassed, the clutching me afterwards, although I knew by then it wasn't me he was clinging to. It wasn't me he'd been attracted to, no, of course not, how ridiculous, it was what he thought was passing through me, that dazzling thing that made his boyish eyes sparkle looking up at me, as though I were a bean stalk suspended from midair. But no one looks that way at a bean stalk. No one looks at you with eyes like that unless they think they can get to something through you, unless they think you point the way to a pot of gold, even believed the gold was already dripping through you, like sap.

In the bathtub, after he'd gone, I'd fallen asleep, and dreamed. And in that dream I was walking along an athletic court of some kind, sand it was, outdoors, maybe for volleyball. And I'd looked down and seen my thin calves suddenly all tan and buff—an athlete's body. I wasn't wearing any shoes, and my feet were covered in shimmering grit: a sparkling tiara for each one of my toes. There were waiters off to one side by a swimming pool, bending under peach-colored table umbrellas and handing out drinks and sweating profusely. Condensation dripped from the glasses. Pools formed in the crooks of their thumbs. But I ignored all of this, and sauntered away toward a line of canvas beach chairs. I sat, watching a fisherman with his line taut out in the surf, reeling it in and then feeding it out, moving back and forth, in and out of the water, toward the waves and then away from them, running toward his catch and then holding off, like an actor hiding from another actor in the wings.

And then suddenly we were in a hotel room high up in the resort, on a floor attached to a balcony instead of the balcony being attached to the floor (dreams being what they are). The room was a disaster; the maid hadn't been in yet and the sheets were all kinked and knotted, the television hung precariously out of its cabinet like a stone about to drop. I felt myself narrowing, a tightening in my stomach that made my head lower and my knees bend; now I was a football player ready for the perfect kick. I grabbed him and threw him and the welter of sheets didn't hide the mirrored headboard, there were mirrors everywhere now, everywhere, and I made sure, when we got going, as I was gunning him, that I was leaning over far enough so that I could see his face, so that I could see his eyes close and his mouth sag and contort with the pressure of me inside him, me, driving him so hard I pushed him right out of himself and through the mirrors and onto the rocks below, until I'd gone right through him and come out the other side, leaving him the split skin of something I was done needing.

I went into the front room and lifted up the phone.

Paul's voice sang out: "We are trapped!"

I had to take a deep breath. Paul is to brothers-in-law as the cicada is to insects.

"You don't have to shout, Paul."

"But we're being *inundated,* Harry!"

I slid the receiver toward the back of my ear. "Where are you?"

"We're under a gas-station awning. The hail is just pounding down on us. I mean it's just *pounding,* like you wouldn't believe!"

"How far away from the house?"

"I don't know. . . . Maybe fifteen, maybe twenty minutes? Sarah is saying—oh, right, we're at the mini-mart place. Fifteen—Wait. It's slowing down now. It's slowing. It's like pearls. Now we can see. A whole street full of pearls. You mean it isn't hailing there at all?"

"Everything's already blown through here."

He sighed, melodramatically. Brother Vanek likes his experiences intense. He can't help it. He's only twenty-five.

"Harry, what happens if we are blocked by a dam of icy pearls? A whole highway of unleashed pearls!"

"Honey, just drive over them."

Paul was a computer salesman turned camera repairman turned my sister's cameraman and husband, and now, when you asked him, he said he was a minimalist cinematographer—which didn't account for all the cinemascope imagery. What he had most in common with my sister was an endless hunger to do and be something bigger than what he'd just done and been.

"I think we're going to be a little late, Harry. Are your parents mad to see us?"

I wasn't sure how to answer this. "How's Sarah?"

"She's good, she's good! She's saying, you know, if her wonderful kind brother Harry has everything all under control out there, maybe with all this trouble we should just hang around out here for a little while, you know, and grab a hamburger or something?"

I let the roar inside the phone speak for itself.

"Okay! Okay. No problem. She says we're on our way, right now, we'll get there as soon as we can. Don't you worry, brother Harry, we're coming to your rescue, we're your knights in shining armor, w— o— and—it—!"

"Paul? Paul. You're breaking up."

We lost the connection.

· 7 ·

Mama was back in the kitchen, her knuckles slimy with fish oil. I picked up a spare crawfish head and sucked it.

"They're almost here, Ma. Turns out they've pulled over to enjoy a nice hailstorm."

"That much of it I got. He is driving carefully, though, isn't he?"

"Mama, Paul doesn't have enough commitment to get into an accident. Can I help you with that?"

She was struggling with a small fan of bones, and her wrists had buckled, her fingers were slipping. But she waved the knife at me, holding me off. "Tell me Sarah didn't talk on that thing."

"No, Mama."

Her shoulders looked pinched at the back. It made you want to unhook them.

"So why is it you don't buy your fish already filleted?"

"Because I don't like something I can't tell was good and fresh when it died. I don't like trusting other people's handiwork. Will you hand me that bowl of crawmeat?"

"So what, now you're going to stuff the—"

"Have you noticed"—she took the bowl from me smoothly—"how much more settled your sister is now? I didn't hear her once trying to say something over Paul in the background. Things are so much calmer for her now."

"Mama. Daddy is calling for you again. From the bathroom."

"Oh?" She listened.

"He's saying . . . he's saying why don't you bring some of that mudbug meat in there?"

"What? I will not!"

"He's saying—he's saying he thinks the poor thing must be dying of hunger."

"Tell him he can just keep his rice in the water. I'll get to it. How do we even know what it likes to eat?"

"Daddy's swearing again."

"Then go on in there and tell him, Too bad. I can't spare any. Paul eats like a horse, it's like having a big, blond Lipizaner in the house, and tonight all I wanted—I wanted—" She coughed, exasperated. "You wait here, I'll tell him myself. Since he's being so *urgent* about it."

She stretched out her hands. Like a boxer testing his tape. Then she turned and washed at the deep sink, dried off her hands, pulled off her *The Chef Is Within His Rights* apron, and brushed past me and under the piece of seine netting tacked over the entry to the back hallway. I watched as she craned her neck around the bathroom door.

"What is it now?"

A low, sharp sound, like cawing. A faint, protesting screeching. Then a vague rustling. Then suddenly, the sound of wildly churning water, muffled profanities, a clattering, along with smacking sounds, strugglings, splashings, hittings, flappings. Mama started forward, her knees buckling out from underneath her like a stack of cardboard boxes falling apart, but smoothly, even while she was coming apart she was smooth, slamming the bathroom door behind her. Whatever tantrum my father was raising inside, she quickly cut it off.

· 8 ·

Why are you two just sitting there, like a pair of zombies, whining, panting up at me from the kitchen floor, waiting for whatever's put down in front of you?

Terriers. It means earth dogs. Earth dogs are not supposed to beg for scraps of crawfish meat.

Now, let me tell you a story. . . .

My father had once begun in this way, pushing our Kool-Aids aside on the long mahogany dining table at the big house. Let me tell you about the nature of the *dog:* he can't really focus on anything except one thing at a time.

Once upon a time, now, there was a boy who lived along the Texas Gulf Coast. Like many humble people at that time and in that place, he had a gun that he used for hunting. Understand, a gun is a terrible thing, chickadees, when it's used for the wrong reasons—for example, when it's turned against a soul that not only wants to but knows why it needs to live. But when it comes to hunting game, and helping bring dinner to the table—well, you have to understand this boy's family was struggling, back then, there was the Depression, you see, and in such cases a gun is absolutely indispensable. Which means, children, it's necessary, and nothing else can take its place.

It was the boy's first gun, a .410, small and slightly nicked but still trustworthy. Now, as it turns out, one day the boy called to his hunting dog, an old black Labrador mix with one blind eye, who was starting to lose his footing when it came to jumping over rocks and sand but still had good enough reflexes for the shallow tidal flats. In those days, there were small duck blinds set out in the bays, bulks of wood and tar that looked like boats half sunk: disguises. So you didn't have to wait very long, peeking out of the hole in one of these, before a flock of small birds started lighting right there in front of you, on the green water. When this happened, the boy fired instantly, and the teal he clipped dove down the way it should right under the water. The dog went in, bucking and bouncing like a jalopy, and then he went straight down too, disappearing through a halo of bubbles. That was his job. He was going for the bird.

After a while, the water went still. The sky went as empty as glass. The other birds had all swung away and headed for the channels, where other people waited for them. The only sound that morning was a thin buzzing hovering over the surface of the water, like a million tiny teeth gnashing.

When too much time had passed the boy realized his dog wasn't coming back up again. He must have gotten caught in some weeds at the bottom, or drowned in some submerged tackle. But there was no point in crying over it. A boy took whatever happened to him, in those days. He took whatever happened and swallowed it whole. Times were so hard for everyone, you see. So this boy dragged his waders through the sand and started sadly for home.

Up ahead on the shelled road he spied a humped, legless shape, dragging itself slowly. Filthy. And black. Its head and body were down low, exhausted, it was rumping its way back from the water, digging its paws in, it was pulling something away from the tide's edge. Now, this boy, he jumped, he ran forward, he shouted, excitedly, he raced and fell and landed next to his dog, happy, so happily, but still careful not to touch its matted head, because its jaw was set and its one good eye was yellow, rolling to one side, looking at the boy, but not loosening on the catch, which was a gleaming redfish, one of its eyes still bulging, face up, its body being wrestled by its huge tail, so big it looked like an anchor in the dog's mouth.

When the dog finally let go, the boy was able to pat the dirty old head, and praise it—because what could it know, it only understood its job was to go down and come back with something, and besides, a redfish the size of a cat was nothing to pass up for dinner—and so he hoisted the fish home in his arms and heaved it onto the cleaning trough. The boy slid his gutting knife up the white belly. And out slid the shimmering blue teal.

I pulled my Kool-Aid back to my chin and stared at my father.

"Did that happen? To you?"

"It did, son."

"It isn't made up?"

"No, son. Not unless made up means told the best way."

"But I don't like it." Sarah blinked from inside her padded helmet and chin guard. "The duck couldn't breathe in there, and it would have been all crusty and slimy inside it."

"The duck didn't know that, chickadees. It was beyond consciousness."

"You're sure?" I asked.

Jean had smiled and told us not to worry and to finish our potatoes.

I gave the dogs niblets out of a bag of food I found sagging in the corner of the kitchen and left them to puck their stainless steel bowls around the floor. The bathroom door was still closed. I waited for a minute, listening, but heard nothing and so went back out into the front room and one by one began cranking at the handles under the windows, rolling up the metal shutters and getting in the last of the sun before it dropped over the shoulder of the coast. It broke like a projector's beam through the dust and dog hair wheeling over the furniture.

I straightened out and plumped all the cushions. I turned and closed the doors on my father's study, ruffling one of the yellow legal pads he used for his rough drafts where it lay, tossed across his desk. The old electric sweeper was in the corner, so I switched it on and nosed it around the room. At least if you're going to have a gay son, chickadees, let him be handy.

Without any warning Mama walked right in front of me. I jumped back and switched the motor off. The front of her T-shirt was soaking wet.

"Everything all right, Mama?"

She ignored my question, and pointed at the vacuum. "Trying to tell me something, dear?"

"Not directly."

"Isn't that sweet of you. Did you hear? Their car is finally pulling under."

"Are you sure? I didn't hear anything."

"You couldn't, you had the duster on." She wiped at her chest, as if to roll the damp off.

"But you heard it?" I asked doubtfully.

"Honey, you know the house always rumbles a little whenever one of you two pulls under."

She was ready by the sliding glass door, with one hand on the latch, the other relaxed and resting against her wet culottes. I heard Paul's tramping on the stairs. Mama was sliding the door back. And now here they were, letting the sand in, stomping, dumping dirt all over everything I'd just spruced up. Paul dropped a frayed backpack and set his camera case down next to it, and then another heavy-looking duffel he pulled from his shoulder. Sarah stood, white chin up, like a statue holding a flame, balancing a plant high over her head, busy keeping it away from the jumping dogs—who had suddenly transformed into a pair of insane, high-maintenance poodles.

"Boys, calm it down, calm it. Mama, I'm sorry it took us so long to get here." She brought the red-flowered plant down to her chest. "Here, a little cacti for you, I thought you might like something succulent for the deck. Say, you look a little succulent yourself. What's been going on around here?"

"Nothing, dear. Isn't this nice?" Mama took the gift. "Paul, would you slide that door closed, dear?"

He did, with a dramatic flourish. "And now we've arrived!"

My sister bent to the dogs to rub their ears and then shoo them away. Her freckled cheeks looked newly carved. Thin. Her latest experiment in hair art was a purple bob with a gash of white through the bangs. Mama, staring, had no chance to comment because Paul was already wrapping his arms around her. In the beginning, this had been the strangest, the most unbelievable part—Paul planting two kisses on each side of her face, Mama holding herself firmly, politely: the seasoned athlete putting up with the greenhorn.

I pointed at the potted plant. "Well, this is darling of you, darling."

Sarah stood. "So you didn't think of bringing anything? Where are your manners?"

"Mrs. Jean! Mrs. Jean!" Paul interrupted. "Did you know that part of your sign, downstairs, it's been blown away, by the wind? All it says now is 'Trespassers Be.'"

"Oh well now." Mama shook her head—generously, I thought. "*That's* not right."

"Paul, sweetheart? Why don't you go on upstairs now—you

remember where my room is, from last time, don't you?—and take all these things up for us. Wait, no, let's give sugars to Harry first." She took hold of my collar, pulling my ear to hers, one nautilus sounding out the chamber of the other. Our usual greeting.

"You okay?" she whispered. "How's it been?"

"You finally got here."

"That bad?"

"Not more than usual."

She smiled and let go of me and turned in the direction of Paul. "Give sugars to Harry, sweetheart."

"Brother Harry!"

"Hey, Paul."

He slid his soft boy's hand over mine, folding my fingers in, holding me there, for a long, long minute, all the while giving me one of his deep, excited, meaningfully intense looks. Too much work. I got myself free.

"Your hair's longer, Harry?"

"I know it. I'm going for the gladiator look."

The sun was piercing the last of the clouds. That was what made his blond hair look like the brightest thing in the room, I thought, what had turned the whites of his eyes into swimming bubbles. Poor Paul. His eyes were too big for his face. Too round and too bulging. Fish eyes. Or maybe he was just spending too much time pressed up against a viewfinder.

"So where's Daddy?" Sarah turned. "Snorkeling?"

This is the way we do it. We joke. Banter. Tease. Frown. Brush off. Call down all the flatness out of the sky, if we have to, imitate the rising moon with its single, yawning expression.

"Your father is with a Booby in the bathtub," Mama explained.

"If he's on top of that, then," Sarah said without missing a beat, "we'll go on up and unpack. Get everything for us, sweetheart?"

"Yes, sweetie." Paul reached down.

"Oh, now." Mama held her hands out. Her sense of fairness had obviously kicked in. "You don't have to worry about all your things right this second, do you? You just got here. Just let be, for a second."

"Tell you what, Mama. *You* all let be. I'm checking out this Goony situation."

"Booby, honey," I corrected.

"Which bathroom?"

Mama waved her hand around the corner. "Down."

My sister's exit meant the three of us were left to stand in the middle of the room, on the creaking floor, shuffling the fresh sand under our feet. Mama looked at me, smiling, and the message for me in her gray eyes was clear: I hope you're planning on helping out with this boy. I have other fish to fry.

"Daddy's got a heron in the hamper," Sarah announced, coming back.

"*Not* a heron." My father followed her in, touching the paneled wall for balance. His shirt was wet and wrinkled as though something had clawed the front of it. "Jeanie? I did put him in the laundry basket, though. To make him more comfortable while he—recovers." He raised his chin, defensive. "I was only trying to toughen him." Then he saw Paul. "Ah. So here is our Mr. Vanek."

Paul reached out his hands, warmly. "It's so good to see you again, sir!"

"Yes, thank you."

"I'm taking the poor thing upstairs right now," Mama said.

"But Jeanie, shouldn't we offer him something to drink, first?"

She rolled her eyes, passing over this, turning quickly to Paul. "Don't you listen to him, dear. You know we don't keep much in the way of alcohol at the beach, but maybe a little beer?"

"Mama," Sarah interrupted. "You know Paul doesn't drink. Are you forgetting?"

Her swollen knuckles tapped the side of her head. "It's getting worse."

Alcohol is never a good idea for epileptics, but it was Paul who seemed to be almost excited by all this teetotaling, nodding his head vigorously now as if being attached to, held back by my sister's routines was a privileged adventure. Sometimes I thought he might be primarily attracted to her for her drama.

My father made his way over to his favorite chair, the wicker squeaking under him as he sat. He kept his back to the window, squinting away from the light. "Tough drive, I heard."

"Oh yes, yes!" Paul dropped across onto the sofa. "A little challenging! But that's what they say about Texas, isn't it, you get bored with the weather, then just wait one minute. In this case, we were obstructed by the forces of an angry ice goddess."

"Really," Daddy said blandly.

"But don't worry, sir, because the weather report I heard for tomorrow is supposed to be excellent. Which means everything will be perfect for the shoot. It will be beautiful. Truly. This sea light is so loaded." And with this he sighed and looked out the window.

"It's going to be just dandy, Daddy." Sarah sat on the sofa, too. "And then we can call it a wrap."

"Wonderful, chickadee."

"You should see what I have so far."

I sat on the ottoman in the corner to keep an eye on my sister. What was she cooking up? I wondered. What was she seeing outlined, around our father, with all that bright, fading light behind him? In those tufts of white hair standing up like wisps of smoke, those grizzled knees under his shorts, those white socks, and those square white shoes, and that fringed shawl hanging next to him—he fussed with it now and pulled it over his lap, covering his bare legs—and that flickering light behind his ears? It made him look, it made the old man look like, well, either the Golden Mask of Crete, or a fool with his bells on, or both.

"I'll bring us some iced teas." Mama turned. "After I've given that poor silly bird something to eat."

"Be sure he's comfortable, Jeanie. Will you?"

She was already around the corner.

He beckoned to us when she was out of sight. "Come closer."

He added after a moment: "I'm going to give you all a little lesson in courage."

Paul straightened excitedly. Sarah and I, casual, didn't move.

"She's always like that, Daddy," my sister finally tossed out, brushing at the throw pillow next to her. "She's unstoppable."

"True. But."

He kept his ear cocked to one side, listening, apparently, in case she came back in. He was wheezing slightly. "She's amazing. I know that. I know. Amazing. But I also want you to know something else. She's swimming through pain. I expect you don't recognize that. She could still do anything, of course. I'm not saying she couldn't. If she wanted to, she could still scale a mountaintop.

But it's only for as long as, as long as—What I mean is, she says it feels like she's having to fight her way through a sheet of pain. That's why I wanted to drop a word in your ear about courage. I needed to stop and make sure. That you understood. Because if you don't see it, if you don't know her by now, then you're not looking closely enough." He stared down at his fingers, flitting in his lap. He stilled them by reaching for his glasses and putting them on again. "A champ, that's the only word for it. A true champion. She deserves something really special tonight, don't you think, children? So what I'm proposing, chickadees, what I am suggesting, since we're all here, and since you all are so clever, and since we have the assembled genetic wisdom of no less than two continents in this room, what I'm suggesting is that we all use the brains that were so generously passed on to us, and be extra *sweet* tonight, perfect angels, as if our butts depended on it. All agreement. Yes? All affinity. And I'm not going to ask a single thing for myself."

"Of course not, Daddy," Sarah said.

Paul bit his soft underlip, exhaling. "Of course, of course!"

"Total bullshit," Sarah said, unpacking. "It is going to end up being all about him, somehow, you watch. He's probably already thinking about priming his ideal dinner audience."

I leaned in her doorway. Her bedroom was in worse shape than mine, her mattress on the floor, made up with an old, quilted spread, the stuffing worked into atrocious pockets.

"But Harry, you know that big gorgeous head of his? It films *beautifully*."

Paul didn't say anything. He was busy putting his shorts away on the single shelf behind him. And this, I thought, this must be the mystery to end all mysteries. Why anyone would ever want to stick his head into another family's damp closets. Unless, like Timothy, he had ulterior motives . . .

"I don't like the way he's letting himself go, though." Sarah handed a skirt over to him. "No excuse for that."

"It's the diuretics, Sar. They just aren't enough anymore to keep the fluids out of his—"

"And you know what else? He's *jumpy*. Fidgety. Did you notice that? All that twitching and flinching and the twiddling his fingers. Pulling that little shawl over him. Was that to get our attention? Come on. They're both of them good for a while yet."

She sighed and dropped down onto her bed, deflating suddenly, her bobbed hair hiding her eyes, her hips sinking into her jeans—she simply vanished, into an abstraction. Gone off, maybe, to watch moving pictures inside her head.

She came out of it, eyes widening. "Why not? I could get that shawl on tape. It's the right touch."

"So is everything all right out your way?" I changed the subject.

"Fine. Austin is Austin. What's up with you? You look thin enough to thread, Harry. It's not—you know." She waved a hand vaguely.

"Don't talk coy. I'm good. I'm fine. And don't talk to me about looks. Your hair, please? Did you lose at paintball?"

"What about yours? Don't you ever sleep with a good stylist? Are you seeing anybody right now?"

"Not at the moment."

"Excuse me, please," Paul whispered, and brushed past me,

scraping my shoulder on his way out to the landing, his face for an instant so close to mine I thought I could feel his breath on my cheek.

He went down to the loft bathroom and locked himself in.

I turned back to my sister, blinking.

"Ah—are you and Paul doing all right? The married life still miraculous?"

"No. You'd be surprised at how ordinary it can be—comparatively." She nodded in the direction of the downstairs. "Why we couldn't just meet in the city again is what I'd like to know. Why is it we all had to come out here this time? Things would have been so much easier at the big house. So much easier on *them.* They have all the help they need over there. Why don't they ever bring any out here, you know? You know these things are going to drive me batty." She squinted up at the whirling ceiling fan. "I could think more clearly if it didn't hum so much here. Have you been working?"

"Yes."

"Anything good?" She looked competitively at me out of the corner of her eye.

"I don't know."

She nodded. "Multiple projects, multiple projects, that's what I'm all about now, Harry. It's the only way to go. And you know film as a form really lends itself to that. I've got all these projects in various stages of development. Lots of interest, too, and not just in Daddy's thing. I have my ear to the ground now; I'm starting to hear more."

"It sounds wonderful."

"To be honest, I really think things are finally coming together for me." She looked down at her freckled hands resting on the thighs of her jeans, palms up; they did look like speckled leaves, turned over. "Crystallizing, you might say."

"That's really great, Sar."

"And there's more. But you'll have to wait and see." She smiled, mysteriously, tossing her bangs. "I have a sense I'm on the right track. I do. And I'll say one thing for me, Harry: maybe I've been overextended in the past, maybe I've been almost *over*-focused, but now I've gotten ahold of something really worthwhile. Of course, I have to finish off Daddy, first."

· 9 ·

The scene: An empty studio apartment. In a city, at night. A small galley kitchen is visible stage right. Down right is a dining table with four chairs, and down left a straight-backed sofa and two more chairs. The strongest light is on the bed at center stage and on a set of half-empty bookshelves rising behind it; two lamp tables finish the bed on either side. More light, white, neon, comes in from a pair of high windows or, if theater configuration permits, a set of skylights. Upstage left a door half open reveals a bathroom sink.

Stage left, a couple enters. Confetti clings to their winter coats. Patches of ice, salt, or snow are sticking to their hems. The first actor is carrying a large green bottle of wine, not new but dull with fingerprints. He crosses and sets it on the dining table, then shrugs his coat off, leaving it on the back of a chair, and crosses up and goes into the bathroom and shuts the door. The second actor, with the same carelessness, takes her coat off and tosses it over the arm of the sofa. She reaches for a television remote, and for a moment blue revolving light floods the stage. Just as quickly, she switches it off. Offstage, sound of a toilet flushing.

The dialogue is minimal and totally improvised. We hear a mumble as the first actor comes out of the bathroom wearing a pair of long, sagging pajamas. The second actor offers a short, mumbled response. She crosses to the bathroom and audibly locks the door. The first actor sways near center stage, as if drunk; suddenly he crosses and grabs the bottle of wine and goes to the kitchen, pokes around noisily and fishes a glass out of the sink. After another moment, he reaches in and pulls another glass out. Carrying these he moves to center stage, pauses, then drops down tired onto the left side of the bed and slouches, staring at the floor.

The second actor emerges in a pair of identical oversized pajamas. Another mumbled exchange as she passes him, crosses, and sits on the right side of the bed.

They slump with their backs to each other. A current should be palpable between them, but weak, sagging between their bent heads. More improvised dialogue now, and mumbling, disagreement or assent. A halfhearted gesture is made by the first actor, holding up the bottle of wine and glasses. She shakes her head no. The clock in the kitchen strikes softly. The first actor sighs, slides the wine and two glasses onto the bookcase that serves as the bed's headboard, then untucks and twists and slides down under his blankets. After a beat, the second actor does the same. They both reach a wide-sleeved arm out—each should look like a white flag stretching from the side of the bed—and switch their respective nightstand lamps off.

Now all is quiet. A single shaft of light from above illuminates the bookshelf and the wine bottle still standing upright on it; but nothing else. All is darkness. We hear the wail of a siren in the distance. The howling of a dog. An indistinguishable white-sleeved arm reaches up from the center of the bed. It finds the wine bottle, grips its neck, turns it over, revolves it, and holds it for a moment. Then brings it down sharply. We hear a loud *thunk* in the darkness. Curtain.

It was my first one-act play in graduate school. Walking after in the darkness under the trees near Washington Square, my father shook his head and said he was sorry, but he found it all pretty shapeless and one-dimensional.

"A play without written dialogue—it's your work, fine, go on ahead, son." He shoved his hands deeper into his pockets. "But you can't really expect it to *say* anything."

Mama caught up to us, having stayed behind to talk to one of her old golfing partners.

"Small world." She pressed her chin into her muffler. "Jason has a son enrolled here, too. Two years now."

"Daddy," I kept on, "think about it. Just think about how it all depends on how the actors improvise. Even on their body types.

On their voices. Their races. Their genders. Tonight, you witnessed just one possibility out of thousands."

"It was that, I grant you."

"What it is, is, I set the basic structure but then relinquish total control. I'm trying to subvert the paradigmatic role of dramaturge."

"Well that lasts about as long as the water stays hot. Tell me, are all of your seminars like this?"

We'd reached the car. "It's no biggie if you didn't like it, Daddy."

"It's not a question of like, son. It's really not enough, in the end, liking."

"*I* did," Mama smiled while he got the keys out, bringing her shoulders up to her neck, stretching. "I liked its decisiveness. It gave me goose bumps, in the end."

My father waved an arm before opening the car door. "But you can get the same effect just standing out here in the cold! And what's more, people don't have to spend their hard-earned nickel for the privilege, or even be bothered to put on clean socks. And *that's* what you have to keep in mind, Harry. That's what you have to ask yourself, day after day. Is it worth someone putting on fresh socks?"

He was obviously disappointed. But something else, something more, some new tone had crept into his voice. I saw a twitching at the back of his collar. He seemed . . . fretful.

By the time we were in our seats he was himself again.

"What a waste"—he sighed and shook his head, looking back at me, smiling—"all this university training ends up being. You know, you'd be better off just running up a stack of unpaid library fines, the way I did when I was in my twenties."

"Don't you pay any attention to him, dear. It's never a good idea to do anything underhand."

"Now, Jeanie, you know as well as I do they have a portrait of me on the wall of that library now."

"More proof, dear, that goodness isn't rewarded."

But I was still wondering about that fretful twitching, leaning forward in the backseat and curious to see if I couldn't get it going again, prod him into forgetting his own work long enough to wonder if his son really had any in him, if his boy had any chance of making it in the world.

"Daddy's right," I said into his ear. "Only talent is."

The three of us went to dinner uptown but had a hard time keeping the conversation going, with all the interruptions, people bubbling up to the table, recognizing him. Being the child of a white-haired Southern icon is like floating face-up in a punch bowl, Sarah once told me. Everyone wants to dip in.

"All I'm saying," he went on when all of this had subsided, "is that it might be good for you, Harry, and for your work, too, if you had a partner, at your back. Some nice girl," he said, pointing with his steak knife, "someone who would really *care* for you. It's worth more than gold, I tell you, having your own Jeanie. I wouldn't be a thing without her."

"That dog won't hunt." Mama reached for the pepper. "I take no credit for what you do, Dee."

"It's so important to have someone you can trust, son. Someone who understands you, who accepts who you are, what has to be done, who can be unfailing—that's all anyone needs, really, but an artist, especially, Harry, an artist, he needs someone to take on half of the minutiae of life. So that his mind and hands can be free to grapple with the wild reins of inspiration."

"Not that you and Sarah were ever minutiae!" Mama looked up quickly.

"Well no of course not." He smiled happily. "You are my sun and moon, you chickadees. But that's the point. Every parent wants to see his children . . . his children . . . anchored. Taken care of. Because, because . . ."

Because life could be such a hard row to hoe alone, he said. Because there were so many things *stuffed* into it, so many cares, and responsibilities, and duties, and problems, and all manner of worries, and all right, even if they ended up being *nice* worries, and even important ones, still, these things could accumulate slowly, stealthily, like drops of rain globbing onto a blade of grass—until finally they stuck in one big heavy globe at the tip and toppled the poor thing over, no matter how bright and sharp it thought it was.

"And after all, don't you want someone to share things with you, and take care of you, Harry, when you're older? In your waning years?"

"Maybe when the time comes I'll just do like you two always said you would, and wait for a hurricane and plant my chair on the beach."

Mama shook her head, laughing. "Harry. We didn't *mean* that."

The next day she and I had lunch together while my father met with his new producers. We went out shopping together, although she wasn't much one for accessorizing. "You know," she said as we came out onto the avenue again, "you don't have to pay attention to what anybody else imagines for you, Harry. It's all a question of personal decision."

"Mama. What are you talking about?"

"I mean"—she stared fixedly at the mannequins in the windows—"it's such a private affair, living. What everybody else does is their own private affair."

"I already know that, Mama."

"You just watch your health, all right, and respect your body? You know what I mean, dear. You *know* what I'm getting at. Harry? Please? Be careful? You *are* being careful, dear?"

I wasn't going to come out in front of Bloomingdale's just like that, just because someone in my family, someone had finally acknowledged what had been perfectly obvious for years. I wasn't just going to toss it off, something so precious. Something that salted away.

"And don't worry about what your father says, you know, I think half the time he doesn't realize what he's saying, he talks out of the side of his head, poor dear, and he's still so *country,* in some ways. And Harry, would you please stop that nail biting, the body is an island, you know that, you wouldn't go around tearing off prime real estate on Pebble Beach, would you?"

"No, ma'am."

"All right, then." She stopped in the street and was fixing her gloves over her large, square hands. "You're going to be just fine, aren't you?"

I blurted out, "I don't know how on earth you ended up with him."

"You should have seen that swing."

We walked on, sometimes separating in the crowd and then drawing close together again.

"I'm waiting," I said when we were held up at a curb, "for someone to make a fool out of himself over me."

"Well of course you are, dear. That's how it should be, shouldn't it? All I can tell you is it's a mess, at first, but then suddenly, it's brick-and-mortar, and you can't tell who's holding up the roof. Now." She cut herself off, embarrassed at having said so much, I think, and stared hard at the lapel of my worn coat. "We need to do something about *this.* I bought Sarah such a nice leather coat when we saw her back a few weeks ago. You're going to get something nice, too. How about in here?" She turned and pushed through the set of revolving doors.

And I remember thinking, as we parted between the panels of glass: maybe love wasn't really a giving of yourself, but finally a holding of yourself off. Maybe that explained it all. It was a kind of keeping at bay. A reserving of strong emotions, you left them in trust, put them by, a capital that couldn't actually be spent. Maybe love casually spoken, doled out too freely between people, in heaping scoopfuls, could be dangerous, even if you craved it—too much of it too rich. Like giving a man starving on a desert island a pound of steak. Maybe love could—it seemed true enough anyway these days—even kill you. Reckless love in the end being the same thing, if you weren't careful, as putting a gun to someone's head.

· 10 ·

For dinner at the beach house we generally comb out our hair, scrape the sand out from between our toes, and go into our closets and pull out something clean. Things, after only a few hours, can already feel brined and clammy. Sarah and Paul had changed into cargo pants, their baggy pockets hanging down in expectant folds of skin. They were standing at the end of the loft, in the doorway of our parents' bedroom, looking in.

"He's just *sitting* there." Paul shook his head. "Not even trying to get out of the box."

Sarah said, "Let's just put him out of his misery. Wring the poor thing's downy neck."

"No!"

"Paul. She's joking."

He flushed. He didn't seem to know, like the rest of us, how to be offhand. He had an unexpected way of becoming embarrassed and confused whenever anything dramatic turned out to be ordinary. He'd hardly been able to get the words out when we'd asked him to explain how his family had escaped Communism. Oh no, no, really! There was nothing to it at all, he'd actually hung his head and stammered. Nothing, nothing worth repeating—only that he and his brothers and sisters had thought they were going on vacation away from Prague, and didn't know their parents had hidden money and their identity papers under the car battery. All they did was cross the border, through Austria into Italy, and then after a while in an Italian camp flew to Canada, it was nothing, really, and in the end all they did was miss by a year the wall coming down.

"Sitting and doing nothing." Sarah sighed. "That bird has poor time-management skills, if you ask me."

The Booby had folded its beak in toward its neck, and almost kinked itself in a knot.

Paul's bulging eyes made my own eyes hurt. "Does, does it think it's invisible?"

"I think it's just flabbergasted," I said. "Sar, close the door again."

"Why is that?"

"So the dogs can't get to it."

"Jean is calling us for dinner!" Paul announced excitedly.

We all went down.

The kitchen was a battlefield, pots and puncture-riddled steamers thrown all over the counter. Mama waved us toward the dinner table. She didn't want any help, she said. "Sarah, Paul, you sit down, on that side, and Harry, you go across from Paul. Dee, get on in there."

My father was busy squeezing in at the foot, guiding the dirigible of his stomach into place. The edge of his place mat was decorated with two pills. Mama's had her three. Willie and Able were prowling around underneath. Mama ordered them to sit, too, and brought over the salad bowl, carrying it in her forearm like a discus. Paul tried again to help. "No, just sit down, dear, and be comfortable, would you?"

My father said, when we were all in our chairs, "Let's take our little moment." He bent his head.

I wondered if Paul—if Sarah had explained it to him—realized this wasn't Grace.

When we were small, my sister and I used to chant a few bumpy words along with our nanny, in memory of our dead Baptist mother:

Bless us O Lord
And these Thy gifts
Which we are about to receive—

Later on Jean had taught us to whisper the words instead of shouting them, since religion was the most private of private affairs, but it wasn't until Sarah's seizures grew gigantic that we gave up on praying altogether. One night she'd fallen from her strapped chair before anyone could catch her, and hit her head twisting between the table's legs. After we'd all gone together to bring her home from the hospital, we sat around the mahogany again, glumly, the spears of the chandelier dangling over our necks, Sarah wearing her new helmet and chin guard. None of us had wanted to say anything. So we simply sat, catching our breaths. And ever since then we've observed this one straightforward moment of silence before dinner. Nothing spoken. Just a lapse. A kind of reprieve. One minute finished, the next one not yet started.

"All right," Mama said. "Eat up, now."

"Jean!" Paul reached over. "This stuffed fish looks so wonderful!"

"Thank you, dear."

"Try some of Mama's special lemon sauce." Sarah handed him the boat. "It's good for a pucker."

"It might grow your beard," my father offered.

"Paul, dear, you just have as much as you like. There's more than I know what to do with."

"Did you always like to cook like this, Mrs. Jean?"

"I didn't start out this way, no. But I do like it now."

Daddy was lifting a chevron of white fish with his fork. It crumbled before he could get it into his mouth. He stared at it a minute, blankly, before coming to himself.

"Why again is it you two can't stay longer, Sarah? I don't understand. One night isn't very much for a visit."

"I wish we could stay longer, sir!" Paul said eagerly.

"You said you had to see about something?"

"We have a few things to see to, Daddy. I'll tell you all about it later."

"I just can't imagine how we're going to have time to do—to get done—everything we need to do."

"Daddy, will you just relax, we'll squeeze it all in. Don't you want me to get back home and get started on your editing?"

"You mean you haven't started yet," he blinked.

She sat back, calmly, wiping her mouth with her paper napkin. "Dad, I told you. I need a little bit more than we've gotten out of you so far. That's why we brought the camera down again."

He turned. "Jeanie, you see how my children work so slowly? Sisyphus has a better record." He sank back in his chair. The wind was blowing in gusts against the darkened window behind him, rattling it. "Well. At least I know my chickadees are well taken care of."

Sarah said, "And we sure do appreciate it, Daddy."

I reached for more of Mama's dirty rice. "It keeps you from fretting, doesn't it, Dad? The trusts being set up and all."

"I'm not sure I'd go that far. A parent always worries."

"Don't you ever worry it might create problems, too?"

"What problems, son? What do you mean?"

"Honey attracts the flies."

"Luckily," Sarah said, "I know how to keep the flies off."

"Harry, dear," Mama put in, "give the money to charity, if you want to, or leave it all be, where it is. It's just meant to be a safety net. Now, you all stop fussing with your food and eat. Paul, more rice for you?"

"Yes, please!"

My father was still bumping his fish around his plate. "Poverty. Poverty, let me tell you, son, that's something you don't need to experience, that's something if you find it dangling over your head too soon, you never grow tall enough to clear it. There was a time, in this very house, when our people didn't have two beans to rub together." He slid his fork under his baked tomato. "Money isn't even enough, in the end. That's why we raised you two up to be sturdy."

Sarah raised one eyebrow at me.

"So, chickadee, can I expect to see that edit soon?"

"All in good time, Daddy."

"All in good time. Well. Just so I know I didn't come off sounding like some—some fossilized goat."

Paul looked up startled from his plate. "A fossilized *goat?* Oh no! That really *was* a concern? Then that means I'll have to go back and check the footage!"

We broke out laughing. Paul Vanek had made a joke.

I said, just to keep things rolling, "Well it has to turn out better than that PBS thing."

Sarah held the boat with the lemon sauce suspended one inch over the table. Mama turned away and coughed behind her hand. My father turned away also. It was something we never talked about, the rambling, the disorientation, the general confusion of that interview.

"Luckily, *my* work is going to be completely different, Harry," Sarah went on. "When a director knows her subject, really understands him, the comfort level is so much higher. She'll get the more honest response."

"I thought," I said across to her, "knowing the subject made it harder to be honest."

"You're both wrong," Mama put in smoothly now, pouring herself more iced tea. "I'll tell you what it is. What you see on a piece of film, it might be *true,* but that doesn't necessarily mean it's accurate. Now, you take the first time, for instance, I ever got a good look at my golf swing." She sat back at the head of the table. "Honestly. You could have knocked me down with a feather. I was so herky-jerky and wild, no one would have thought I'd ever make it out of the Carolinas. But in the end, it didn't matter if the camera loved me. I knew what I was up to."

"Yes, that's it, that's it exactly!" My father brightened. "You should have seen her. She was amazing. Glorious. The most powerful thing on two legs." He leaned in toward her. "You were like the universe made visible, Jeanie. Mathematics, physics, the very laws of it. You just reared back and *whaled* on them."

"Get out of here, Dee. You don't even know what you're talking about. By the time we met I was nearly forty, and *well* past it. Besides, what makes you think you could tell the difference between a smart swing and a hot lunch?" She confided in Paul's direction: "My style was called a fire-and-fall-back. Very unconventional."

"It sounds awesome, Mrs. Jean."

"Dear, I know it does, but what with all the technology they have these days, the computer modeling and the who knows what, the trainers probably would have beaten it right out of me. That's the fascinating thing, isn't it?" She looked down at her chest. "You can pretty much do anything you want to, now, with a body."

"Mrs. Jean, do you miss your playing?"

"Oh no, no." She kept her head down.

"Sarah told me your parents started you in the game, is that right? They must have been so *proud* of you! You hit farther than any woman ever hit, back then. I know all about it."

"My parents didn't live to see it, dear. I was adopted, remember, and they were much older people."

"That's right!" He turned to my sister, excitedly. "She was *adopted.*"

"Mama was so good," Sarah changed the subject quickly, "no one could ever say it was her fault Harry and I could never hit past our own feet. You had to give up on us, didn't you, Mama?"

"I don't blame you, honey. I blame your father's example entirely."

"I wasn't *that* bad."

"It's all right, Dee. It's all behind you now."

"Why not a few bunkerless courses, now and then, for variety's sake? That's what I want to know. Would someone tell me that? Why not make things just a little bit easier on the poor, earnest duffer?"

A squeaking sound. It was coming from the fork between Paul's teeth. He was biting down on it, hard, considering the question.

"Well, sir," he broke out, "maybe because, because of, the *boundaries* between things? You know, because it could be like this: sometimes, the more difficult something is that we think should be easy for us, but it isn't, then, the more the difficult things that we think *should* be difficult for us, and they *are,* the more they seem, you know, somehow *right* for us?"

My father's jaw dropped.

"Well, who would have thunk it. The boy has a key in his lock. Good on you, Mr. Vanek. Good on you."

Sarah slipped a triumphant look at me. Paul was looking down, delighted, at his plate, and then he peeked over at me, blushing—one of his intense, meaningful looks. But why blush at me, like that? I stared back at him. Why not send that happy, bashful, awkward look over toward my father? What do you think you're doing?

But I knew what. Paul had been memorizing a scene from one of my father's early plays, one of the most widely successful, controversial dramas of the 1960s—one in which the main character, a mean, shiftless white drifter, who's just killed a black man for looking at a white woman, says in part, in monologue:

> *The fact that we were doomed to lose to Jesus' example, from the beginning, nope, it don't matter to me, it just can't matter to me, no more. Because it was worth it to have fought with something as hard as this was, to have felt myself alive because the beautiful thing I wanted was so strange to me, so far from me, so terrible for me, and yet so necessary to me. And now that I'm sitting here, alone on this ledge, looking over it, I can say I don't regret any of it, no, no, not a lick—because I'd rather have fought with something perfectly monstrous, or monstrously perfect, or even with a cheat that beat me in the end, than with an idea so feeble it gave me every excuse not to whup it.*

Paul was fumbling at me with those bulging, round eyes. I wanted to hit him.

Mama waved her hand over the dishes. "All done?"

"Well, we—" Sarah started. But then seemed to change her mind.

My father's good humor, in the meantime, had evaporated. He was twitching now, frowning, muttering to himself, groping clumsily for a piece of fish on his plate, the loose scrap of skin getting away from him. He finally manged to toss it down to the dogs.

· 11 ·

Mama sent us into the front room for dessert.

"I can't get anything done in a kitchen with this many people in it. Paul, Sarah, go out there and keep your father company. He must be getting lonely now, just sitting under the lamps. Harry, dear, would you wait back and take a few more things?"

She handed me the scalding coffee. "The cups are already out there. Wait, dear, I've got a tray full of ice treats in the freezer. You lead the way, now."

I set the coffee down in front of the sofa. Mama handed around the almond vanilla crunches she was so proud of. From his chair, my father took one look at his ice cream, and then dug into it so hard with his spoon the glass actually squealed. He gobbled as if he were trying to get ahead of something scalding and voracious in his body.

Sarah and Paul hadn't noticed, whispering into each other's ears.

"What's going on?" I interrupted. "Come on, Sar. Give it up, now. You've been acting the big mysterious ever since you got here."

Mama was paying attention now. "What is it?"

Sarah tossed her hair back. "Well, I wasn't going to just *blurt* it out. But since you're getting so anxious, Harry."

Paul sat up wide-eyed, as if at any minute he expected a parade to go by.

"You all don't think I'm going to stand for any gloating, though. You hear me? Any smug I-told-you-so's. Not from any of you. All right? Paul and I are getting ready for a child in our lives."

Something shook the stilts underneath the beach house. A burst of wind, it felt like a train rushing under where there'd been no tracks. The tufts of dog hair in the corners whirled. My parents' faces actually looked blown back.

"What?" my father stammered.

"Don't you go all Barney Fife on me, Daddy. Paul and I have been talking seriously about this, for a long time. And anyway, now we've decided it. It's just the next natural phase for us. It's a conscious choice on both our parts."

"Now?" Mama asked, mouth staying open.

"Chickadee, we mean, we mean—are you certain—? Are you—? Harry?" He turned blankly to me.

I couldn't think of anything to say. My throat felt silted up.

"We're as certain about this as we've ever been about anything. That's why we have to get back to the house, Mama, Daddy, because on Monday, we have to—"

Deep, shaking, full-bellied gusts of laughter. Like a pair of dockyard workers they were now, rollicking, rolling, Daddy's hand reaching out for Mama's square thigh, something I'd never seen before, this unbalanced hanging onto her, grabbing her. "Well, doesn't that just *beat* all!" He was hooting. "Hell and high water are here!"

"Okay." Mama was wiping her eyes, laughing. "I want you both to know *I* never said that."

Sarah waited patiently, folding her arms. "Calm down, now." She looked over at me suddenly. Nervously. "Well. *You* haven't chimed in, Harry."

She was my baby sister. What could I say? I smiled. I bobbed. I nodded. "It's just *great,* Sar." But the truth was, I felt hollow: it was like nodding inside the head of a Chinese dragon. Was I really that puny, I wondered?

My father pulled himself together finally, pressing one hand over his wild eyebrows, and holding out the other to Paul. "It seems congratulations are in order. Well done, son."

My brother-in-law was beaming. "Yes, yes sir, but maybe we should explain—"

"Jeanie, do you know, they don't have a clue, do they?" He sat back down and sighed and shook his head. "They have no idea what an undertaking this is going to be. The raising of children. They can't know it. How the little lions consume everything in the den. Still nothing else matters, as long as you get it right."

"Daddy," Sarah interrupted.

"Now, when *my* little chickadees were born . . ."

The well-worn monologue rolled out. How Harry Buelle had somehow managed to pop out, inconveniently, while everything was still so frenzied with rehearsals in New York—the little tyke hadn't been scheduled to arrive until a good five days *after* the opening. But then on the other hand, when *Sarah* was born—now in that case he'd gotten back, just in the nick of time, and insisted on being taken straight from the taxi into the delivery room, which wasn't how things were done at all, in those days, but he'd bluffed his way in, only to find his daughter all shriveled and shrunken and blue in the doctor's hands. Well! He had nearly fainted. But then everyone else nearly had, too, the nurses half panicked and blanching at him, the doctor smacking and slapping, and all the while Sarah hanging downside up, refusing to take a breath, apparently she was particular about her element, and she just kept on turning more and more purple, more and more like a tight bud rose, until finally, as if on cue, as if she'd only been waiting for the room's attention, she let out a long, earsplitting wail.

He shook his head, wonderingly. "Impossible to explain it. Impossible to describe how everything is in that moment. In that one second, when the breath floods in. Little chickadees." He looked at us. "They're everything."

"Daddy," Sarah said drily.

"And do you know, you know what it is—nobody *tells* you what it's going to be like! Nobody prepares you, Jeanie, for what it *feels* like, holding your own flesh and blood in your hands. Holding your own heart in your hands, that's what it is, that's exactly how it feels, you're suddenly holding *yourself* in your hands, it's all you, all naked and wiggling and slippery."

Sarah said, "Mama, he won't let me finish."

"Finish what?"

"What I'm trying to tell you. We're adopting."

I heard his breath catch.

She reached over to feel for Paul's knee. "It's really a wonderful idea, you know. And it's not like we don't have a history of this in our family." She looked steadily at Jean. "Our plan is to go back to Europe. We're going to visit with some of Paul's family there first. Then we're going to go across and try and adopt a Bosnian orphan, maybe about ten, twelve years old—there are so many of them left there, Daddy. It's terrible."

This was out of left field even for my sister.

"What are you all staring at us for? You're not seriously telling me you have a problem with this?"

"Of course not, no." My father collected himself. "It's fantastic." I watched him, saw him look over his shoulder. *Jeanie? Jeanie?* Mama was keeping her jaw smooth. He turned again, shaking his head, confused, he was trying to catch up, I could see that, he was blinking, trying out this new idea, trying to come around to it, running it through his head, like an untested title: *A Bosnian Comes to Texas.* "So what you're saying, now, is—?"

"I'm saying, Daddy, that we're just not into all this duplicating ourselves everybody else is after." She looked from one to the other of them, deliberately. "And anyway, I hate that after every war people forget. All those children left to fend for themselves. It's not right."

He nodded slowly. "It's just—it's just—But I guess my ears were playing tricks on me."

"No tricks, Dad."

"Are you sure about that?"

She blushed.

"But Sarah, dear, the Bosnians?" Mama put in reasonably. "They don't mind their children leaving? Being taken away from them?"

"And which—*which* Bosnians?" my father realized.

My sister seemed unfazed. "Does it matter?" And she reached down to pet Willie, who had come up and was nuzzling at her feet. "What's wrong with just lending a hand, Daddy? What's wrong with trying to make a better world?"

"Nothing wrong, chickadee."

I was watching Mama now. She was adjusting her arms in her lap. Still trying hard to be fair. "I was adopted," she said smoothly, "and I'm proud of you, we both of us are, dear. You know that. This will really be something special."

I had to duck and reach down and scratch Able, who had come up to me, jealously whimpering. *But this is Sarah we're talking about,* I had to bite my lip to keep from saying to him. We all know her, don't we know all this is nonsense, she won't make it, they won't make it, either one of them, they'll change their minds before they've reached the airport, before they've even made the reservations. One or both of them will lose interest, or want to be a music producer, or who knows what else. Paul, just look at him, was already wandering away in his head, listening to some tune, distracted, looking around the room.

Daddy's eyebrows suddenly shot up. "No!"

"No?" Sarah laughed.

"Dear," Mama said quickly. "Your father's getting a little tired."

"Jeanie"—he turned to her—"something about this isn't obvious."

"What you mean is," I waded in carefully, "Sarah could have made all this a little bit more obvious up front. Couldn't you have, Sar?"

"I don't know. I thought I made the major point early on."

"Is it your health?" my father asked, still confused. "Is that it? Is this in some way connected to your health?"

"That's not it at all."

"But how do you know you'll be able to treat him as your own flesh and blood?"

She tilted her head toward Mama. "You don't think I've had enough experience?"

I looked quickly over at Paul. But it was clear he was completely lost, blinking, an extra blinded by the lights.

"He means do you think you might regret it later on." Mama—perfectly in control. "Missing out on the physical experience?"

My sister picked at her baggy pants. "It's just I don't need to add anything physical right now, to my routine, what with all I have going on, all my work, all my plans. But that's beside the point. Mama. Daddy. You have to be able to see. This is an important project for us."

"A *project?*"

"You never said it that way when it came to one of yours, Dad."

The struggle in his face, the taking it in, the bewilderment, he was all transparent again, the blood siphoning through his cheeks.

Then my sister pushed it too far. "Daddy, some ideas take a little getting used to, don't they?"

All at once he relaxed, his bushy eyebrows going up but the heavy lids coming down. "You're so right, chickadee. I guess they do. And sometimes all that's required is a minute of reflection. Well. I think I'm beginning to understand, now. And we do have to make allowances. Don't we?"

"It's not an allowance, Daddy."

"You're right, it's a terrible waste."

"Dee," Mama said quietly.

Sarah took the bait. "Of what?"

He pointed a finger at her braless chest. "Throwing all that magical marvel away."

In a flash she dropped down cold into her lake. I saw it. I saw her eyes go distant, behind a pane, like a diver's.

Mama turned on him. "Do you know how much like a *dinosaur* that makes you sound?"

I jumped in, protective. "You mean a fossilized goat, don't you, Mama?"

"But Jeanie. I'm telling you. She doesn't understand *who* she is. *What* she is. What her own body is for."

"Oh my God. Can you believe this?" My sister turned to face me, her eyes growing darker. "Can you actually believe what I'm hearing here?"

My father, however, was in his element, sitting back, authoritative, perfectly calm. "You know I hate to say this, dear, but this sort of thing always reminds me of these poor people we run into in Hollywood—doesn't it, Jeanie? The ones who keep running around adopting children, they want so *much* to be good, and generous, and kind, and yet they can't even acknowledge they're doing what comes easily and fashionably, and keeps them skinny, too. And I'll tell you what I always think when I see them like that, chickadee. That I'm witnessing the desperation of dilettantes."

"Dennis."

For an instant my sister flashed her eyes in Paul's direction. "I guess, then, Daddy, Mama didn't go to the courthouse to adopt us because that would have showed everyone she was a—a what? A *dilettante?*"

Mama stood up effortlessly. "Oh, come on now." Nothing about her was even remotely stiff or swollen, at that moment. In her steely eyes I thought I could make out a distant flag she was absolutely sure of. "We're all just crabby, now. You know what I think? We're beyond anything useful at this time of night. Paul, dear, aren't you tuckered out from your long drive?"

"Yes, ma'am!" He stood awkwardly, confused, but smiling and anxious to please. "I do feel a little dizzy, maybe from looking at all the ice in the road. Maybe, sweetie, we should go on upstairs, now? And—"

"Stop patronizing me." Sarah pulled her arm away slowly.

Paul looked for help in my direction.

"Mama's right." I stood. "I'm calling it a night myself." I stretched, for the casual effect. "No use in getting any bitchier. Can I help you with any of this first, Mama?"

"No. Yes. All right," she decided finally. "The rest of you, now, you go on up and get comfortable."

"I'm staying here," my father announced.

"I'm out," Sarah stood.

Mama nodded again. "Yes, dear. You have so much to get rested for, don't you?"

"We see the travel agent on Monday." My sister stopped and looked deliberately at my father before she left. "Mama's right. Paul and I have so much ahead of us."

I came out of the kitchen drying my hands on my shirt to find Daddy had swiveled his chair to face the darkened window. He was staring distracted out into the night, out at the faint, white curls of the waves.

"Are you going to bed now, Dad?"

The dimness made his eyes look soupy. Like oysters.

"I am not."

"You want anything else before I go up?"

"Hand me that magazine over there, before the dogs get to it."

I bent and got it away from Able.

For a second—I couldn't help this—I held it off from him. Like a nanny. "Are you sure, Daddy? Sure you wouldn't rather just go on up to sleep now?"

He stared dully at the pages in my hand. "I sleep down here, son."

"What? Where?"

"I sleep in this chair."

"Why?"

He raised his eyes to me. "Because I don't lie down, anymore, in my own bed. Why, you ask? Because I don't like the feeling of breathing when I lie down. Why? Because it feels like someone's sneaking up and choking me. Now, *may* I have my magazine?"

I let go and he took it and dropped it onto his shawled lap. He looked at me again, without a smile, without a frown, without any expression at all except a sweaty gleam, a kind of rawness.

"Dad—? Daddy, can't I—?"

"Go on." He waved me off impatiently. "Get on out of here."

I turned away. Imagine the heart is something tight and closed, like a tangerine. Now imagine you can feel, inside you, thinly divided segments, tearing.

· 12 ·

At night, after they'd finished a hard day's work, they'd all be sprawled out on the sand, maybe on blankets under the stars, dragging out tins and flasks of Prohibition whiskey and swigging them back and making bad jokes while singing off-key Prohibition songs:

You got to have gravy, baby
Just one bottle more
Oh you got to have gravy, baby
Or shoot me to the floor

Overhead, the beach house stood unfinished, going up in stages, like a barn in the middle of a field. At night they would stop to rest, the friends and neighbors of Patrick and Doris Buelle. The wind had licked over the grasses. The foam on the waves had turned a color that wasn't like any color at all, more like the disappearance of color inside something too fragmented to hold it. They say babies rarely cried, in those days, staying wide awake, crawling away if you didn't catch them by their ankles. Boys came back from the dunes with faces ironed flat, giving nothing away about what they'd just done to each other. In those days the beach was worth nothing, so people had come from inland and squatted along the bays and the rivers. They would have partied all night in the late 1920s; and then, slowly, and then suddenly quickly, there was no more drinking, and no more singing under the stars. The friends trucked away, but the Buelles at least had their shack on stilts when the bank took their real house in town, and luckily a baby could be left upstairs, for a few hours, gurgling in its box, if you had to go out fishing or hunting for your supper.

On one good night, after a good haul of shrimp had come in, my grandparents had decided to celebrate by going to a pier dance. My father remembered clearly being checked on in his trundle upstairs, pretending to be asleep with his book stuffed under his sheets. They whispered to him to be a good boy, and to keep an eye out for more than himself—and that was the last time he heard his parents' voices. The waves, he told us, kept on rolling over and over one another, like one box of ball bearings being slid over the back of another.

In my mind, Patrick and Doris Buelle meant no harm or betrayal. They only needed to let off steam, cut loose, run fast toward the glow of a fistful of lights strung out over the water. On the pier and then inside the dance hall, the crush of people felt numbing, soothing, everybody two-stepping close enough to every other body to know it still wasn't close enough. And all the pounding, grinding music. And the flashing darkness and light. Erotic vibrations coming up through the floor. And the dancing, the dancing, how it got into your blood like something that finally matched it, like something that finally fit, something you hadn't known you'd needed until it was already inside and through you, and then suddenly your body didn't feel like an anchor anymore, no, not at a dance club, but like a suit that had actually been made for you.

The newspapers reported the pier did give a few warning jerks before it went down. It was a headline in this part of the state, still preserved in the town library, with survivors describing how it sounded like a Ford Model T backfiring. The stilts under the hall hadn't been shored up properly. The construction had been shoddy. The lights and live wires had dropped too fast into the water.

Most of the dead were found electrocuted near the dock. A few others, like my grandparents, had been inside, in the wrong place at the wrong time, when part of the hall's roof collapsed, pulled along with the jerking pier like a curtain dragged down by a clumsy orchestra.

Didn't you cry? we asked my father. Daddy, Daddy, didn't you cry?

But times were so hard, you see. You had to swallow whatever happened to you. You had to take the bad with the good. And it was like everyone said, all the time, in those days: Chickens can't stop the sky if it wants more room.

· 13 ·

I twitched awake, sweating. It was all right. I was out from under it. The house was below me again, solid. I had stripped down to my underwear; now I threw the sheets back, hot. Everything was so quiet. So quiet I could feel the weight of the air shoving in from the low-pressure system offshore, feel it leaning, pressing against the other side of the closed door.

Then it coughed.

The moon was so bright at my window I couldn't make out the shadow of sandals or slippers under the doorjamb. Whoever it was there, they hung, suspended, heavy—like an elephant without feet. I swung my legs over the side of my bed. The sound of the surf would cover the springs' squeaking, dive up under me and bear me up like a cork. But then I forgot about the floorboards snapping.

I heard muffled footsteps, shuffling away. I reached the door and opened it. Too late. No one was there. I went out onto the landing and looked around. But the loft was all darkness, and the downstairs was nothing but shadows in pools and bulky, indecipherable lumps.

I slept longer than I meant to. By the time I'd thrown on a pair of shorts and gotten myself downstairs, the kitchen was clean and empty except for Paul, who was wiping the tiled counter around his coffee mug. The dogs had been fed leftovers. They were snoring satisfied next to their bowls.

"Good morning, Harry!"

I felt for my hair, tugging it behind my ears. "You're already on the stuff. I guess everybody got an early start today."

"It's my third cup. Mrs. Jean—your mama? She keeps really good coffee around here."

"You sleep all right?"

"I never get used to the water, Harry. It sounds like a wreck happening over and over." He listened, as if fascinated.

"Where is everyone?"

"Your parents, I think they're still out driving in their golf cart. Sarah's heading over to the wildlife sanctuary. She went in our car."

My hand froze on its way to the coffeepot.

"No, it's all right, Harry, she's driving a lot more now she has a real license. She's so much better these days. These new medications are really something. Mornings especially aren't a problem for her anymore."

I hadn't known this. "That's good to hear."

"Anyway, you know, you just can't stop Sarah from doing what she wants to do. And she wanted to go all by herself."

I filled my cup. "Then that means she's still pissed off at all of us. Did she sleep okay?"

"One small little seizure. Her wrists are a little sore, this morning, from the contraction. But that's all. Harry, you know her, it's no big deal, she's so amazing. You want some breakfast?"

"I don't eat in the mornings."

"I forgot. Well, then, how about we go out, maybe take a little walk, for energy, for air? Go out and find your parents? I don't know, but it seems like they've been gone a long time now. They were in their shoes and windbreakers even before Sarah got up. Your father had rings under his eyes."

"Well I wonder whose fault that was."

He blushed, deeply. "I think, I think Sarah is trying to make up for things last night by taking care of the bird and finding it a home. We didn't want to make anybody feel . . . badly. Really, you have to know that, Harry. But the weird thing is, when I told your daddy what she was going to do, about taking the bird, he only shrugged, like he didn't care about it at all anymore."

"Boobies have that problem." I turned away.

"What problem is that?"

"They wear people out."

Over my shoulder I could sense his hurt eyes following me.

And was ashamed of myself. That wasn't right. It wasn't how I'd meant to be, that morning. I was just feeling bitchy.

I drank my coffee looking out the window and tried to think of something nice to say.

"Harry?" I heard him coming toward me again. "Harry? Are—have you been all right?"

It was no use, it was going to be far too claustrophobic to stay indoors with him. "You know, Paul, I think we should take that walk. Since the weather's being so cooperative, finally."

"Great! I love the *outline* of things so early in the day, don't you?"

We put on our flip-flops and made our way down the stairs, kicking off the dried seaweed clinging to the steps. The salt in the air tasted fresh. The sand in the shade was still wet and brown. The sky was so clear and white. The golf shed had been left with its doors unlocked and swung open; the blue trumpet vines around it were flattened under tire tracks, even though that had always been Mama's pet project, year after year, keeping those blue flowers firm and upright, digging their roots in deeper, if she had to, transplanting them if things looked perilous enough. Because the minute the vegetation line fell back, the minute those trumpets retreated under the house, by law the property reverted to the state, and we would have to pay to have the house moved away or torn down. But that wasn't ever going to happen, my father said. The Buelle family were finally legitimate, taxes paid, no more squatting or sneaking around.

"Such a wonderful breeze." Paul stopped and held out his long arms. "So perfect. And not hot at all, this late in the year."

Farther down, the taller and more expensive houses had already closed their shutters up for the winter and stood like sealed silos. The water edged higher and higher while Paul and I walked, leaving foam and trash in the way ahead of us. The tide was coming in.

"You think, Harry, it's all right your parents went out like this, for so long, at their age?"

I reached down and picked up two halves of a perfect clamshell, closed them, opened them, and let them drop. "My guess is they had to get away from us. I think we turned out to be more work than they expected."

His eyes followed the line of foam. "Have *you* been working hard, Harry?" he asked me blithely. "Is that what's been weighing you down?"

In the sun, his white-blond hair sparkled. His eyes were two transparent eggs. I could see signs of movement inside them, real life. The way I had seen it inside Timothy's. My stomach heaved, and I looked away.

"People talk too much about work, Paul."

"But I like to talk about work! By noon it will be so nice for the shoot."

"You must have a light meter in your head."

"It's not all I have," he said confidingly.

"I think—" I swallowed and kept moving. "I think you two should take it easy, filming my father, later today."

"We will. Don't worry at all. There's not much left for us to do, really. I just want to capture how *strong* he sounds. And a few more good angles. I like him very much, you know."

"Then you have a funny way of showing it." I let that one sink in.

"I just wish," he half-apologized to a wedge of driftwood, "you had any kind of idea how hard it is, sometimes, to know exactly how to behave around all of you."

The clams were sending their bubbles up through the sand. "I have no idea what you mean by that."

"Well, with Sarah, you know? Already, I have to be so careful around her. Sometimes it's like I have to move around her in a big circle."

"You were the one who wanted to marry her."

"She asked to marry me, Harry. And then, you know, your mother and father? I feel that—I just know that all the time I have to watch out, or they'll think I'm some kind of Bohemian freeloader."

I heard Mama's voice coming out of me: "Oh, that's not right."

"Some conversations can be so intimidating. Especially around your father. You know I read his work, when I was in school, in Czech?"

"It's no big deal, honey. I read Ladislav Smocek."

"But Smocek never made it big in Hollywood."

We kept on over a huge bleached log, past sandpipers racing to one side. The space in between us grew wide and then narrow again.

"Your father has done so much in his life."

"I don't know it's all that much. He's not Shakespeare. He's not in Zulu. Get a grip, Paul. What he is, is an extremely good showman, and he knows his audience."

"And what about Mrs. Jean? She can be intimidating, too. I get the feeling she can put you right where she wants to, if she wants to."

I thought back. "Yes, she can," I said.

"But I like her too, you know, Harry? I like strong, tough women. She has hands like a man's. Sometimes I even think I'm looking, you know, at two people, a man and a woman, when I look at her. I don't mean that as an insult." He laughed and slapped me on the back. "You know, under the Soviets, we had some women taking things to be stronger, to be winners. But that's not what I'm thinking about. I mean she's intimidating because she's so natural, and she's just as big as your father, and I know, because Sarah told me, she was a very great player."

I picked up the pace. Somehow it was as if I weren't moving at all, because Paul kept up with me, kept at me, so doggedly, and all the while the waves next to us and all around us were of one and the same piece, an endless, rolling backdrop, so I might as well have been standing in one place, running a heart test on a treadmill.

"Anybody's family can be hard to be around, Paul. So what about me?" I stopped and the wind backed up my hair. "Am I so hard?"

"Oh!" He caught his breath, laughing. "Absolutely. You are the *worst.* You're like somebody who stands in three different places at the same time." He ran his fingers through his own hair. "It's like, one minute you're here, and then you're over there, and then, I don't know, it's like you're some kind of new adaptive computer technique, springing holographs up all over the place. Also, I never know what you're thinking."

"Why should you care what I'm thinking?"

"Because I want to, Harry."

"But why?"

"Because I can't help it." His eyes looked straight into mine. "Because, because I've started to feel so much *closer* to you now . . . because . . ."

His hands were fluttering, touching my arm, awkwardly. We stood swaying a little in the fitful wind. I looked down, and each of my toes was wearing a sparkling crown of sand. I could feel the blood welling up from my feet, being pulled up into my ears. And I heard pounding. And I saw things, undulating. It was like being dragged under water. I saw Paul's plumbed, wet, alive eyes. I looked past them and saw over his shoulder a silver mullet flinging itself out of a wave and slapping itself down, completely out of control. It was all so close. So close. All you had to do was let go, and there you were. And then, what would that be like? But you wouldn't know, would you? You couldn't know, beforehand, because if you tried imagining it beforehand, if you tried thinking too carefully about it, you'd see the blankness, you'd see the wall, and you'd chicken out, you wouldn't go through with it, you wouldn't dare. Only the wanting would be left, stupid, dumb. The buzzing wanting. I stood there, dumbly. My face felt like a hot glowing flat blank, transparent, a scrim lit from behind. I thought, He must be able to read every single thing written across me.

"Paul."

"I need so much to talk to you, Harry."

"Paul. No."

"It's been so hard. *So* hard. Just to begin to try and— And then, of course, Sarah wouldn't approve. She can be so competitive, that way."

I blinked. A gull passed over us and dropped a bright blue-and-white splash on the sand.

"I've just started to feel so much in *common* with you, you know, you and your father both? And all in these last months, too, because I'm finally seeing, I'm finally seeing, the work, the work I'm *really* wanting to do, now. The *real* work. It's the artist's life. I know that it takes years, Harry. That it would mean starting over, in many ways. I do. But I want to be just like you."

I saw a spot on the horizon. It was starting to become clearer.

I pulled my shoulder away from him, casually, turning my head to wring the flush in my neck out.

"And what work is that, Paul?"

"I'm writing now, too, Harry. I want to be a playwright. Like you and Dee." He said the syllable so happily, almost shivering with excitement. "I think it's a better way, you know, into the *heart* of things. And I've already written one play."

"Well, what do you know."

"That's why I needed to talk to you, Harry. I need to show it to him. Soon, I think. There's no time like the present. Maybe, maybe even still this afternoon."

"You can't be serious."

"Why?"

"Why? Would you—*please?*" I stepped away into the water and got my feet clean. "Don't you think you might want to concentrate on finishing one thing before you start another? Don't you think you might want to consider my father? Haven't you noticed anything about him? Anything at all? Don't you think this might not be the best time for another little—surprise?"

He skirted a wave. "I know, I know, that's what Sarah would say too, if I told her. But it is a good thing, trust me." He kept on, carried away. "I think it could even be good for *him,* you know, to know how we're both doing this thing that's so important to him. Carrying it on, in the family. Plus, I don't know how to stop, really, Harry, not now, now that I've found something just for me, just for *me,* to express myself honestly. Don't you think it's important to express oneself as honestly as possible?"

I wanted to hit him again.

"So, anyway, can you please promise to read my play for me today? Soon? And tell me what you think about it? And then, if it's good enough, if I have something you like, then *you* could introduce it to him, for me. It's all in the family, that way."

I pointed in the direction of the growing white spot. "Why don't you just take it to him yourself? Why don't you just tell him about it right now? Don't worry, Daddy's always so receptive to apprentice work. Come on, you can tell him now, they're going to pull right up here."

He was practically hopping with dread, his shorts all bunched in a knot. "No, no, no! I really don't think it's a good idea, in terms of the family politics. Anyway, I need to know if *you* think it's good enough, first. That's so important to me. Really. I need you for my test."

"Is it your first play? Then I can tell you it's shit."

"But you don't even know what it's about!"

"What is it about?"

"It's a *big* subject. Something really important: man's inhumanity to man."

"Really."

"You have to go after something that grabs people by the throat, your father says."

"I know."

"Look, they're coming, now. Harry, let's not talk anymore about this, right now, okay? I'll show you what I have later on. I think you can read it pretty fast. It's not very long, you'll see."

"Just a little inhumanity."

We watched the dome of the golf cart approach us. "I'm not doing anything behind my sister's back," I added quickly. "I want you to know that."

"Of course not!" Paul said excitedly. "Once you think it's good enough, then we can tell her. She thinks so much of your opinion, Harry. She says you look down your nose at everything, so if you like something, it must really be good."

They were pulling up next to us now, the tire tracks behind them filling in like soggy veins.

Mama was at the wheel. Both of them looked glowing, their faces winking with salt and sand.

"What's been going on?" I said. I pointed to my father's reddened cheeks.

"Nothing, son! Just humping and bumping around."

"Nice to see you up, dear," Mama teased.

"You boys need a lift from us?"

How I wanted, how I yearned to be on that cart. But: "Take Paul," I said, perversely. "He's been anxious to see you this morning."

"Oh, sir, no, there really isn't any space! It's only for two people!"

"Anxious? Are you worried about the shoot, son?"

"It's not that." Paul glanced sideways at me, for help.

Mama scraped her hair behind her ear. In that light it looked as tough as leader line. I saw the heel of her hand was purple.

"What's that? What have you been up to?" I said again.

My father raised his hands to the sky. "We've been beyond the beyond! And then back again!"

"Oh, don't listen to him, dears. We've just been down to the mini-mart for Frappuccinos."

"You'll run the battery down going that far, Ma."

"Would you have come looking for us?" my father demanded. "Or would you have waited for our bones to be picked clean by the crabs?"

"Daddy," I pleaded.

Paul grabbed one of the cart's bars, shaking it distractingly. "It's such a sturdy way to get around, isn't it, Mrs. Jean?"

"It is, dear. Very quiet. Like sailing without a sheet. All right then, since Harry is getting so frantic about the juice, I guess we'll head on back in."

"Wait, you've got sand on your chest, Mama."

"Now, I wonder how *that* happened?" She looked down.

"And what about me?" My father stuck his stubbled chin out, jealously.

"You need a shave."

"I know. I'm going back to do that right now." He smiled again and squinted at Paul. "Need to look all spiffy for the last act, don't I?"

"Yes, sir!"

Mama hit the pedal and they hummed away.

"They should have taken the car," I fretted, "if they were going out that far. I don't see why they aren't being more careful these days."

"Maybe it's safer for them not to be on the road?" Paul patted my back, patronizingly. "Maybe you're worrying too much."

· 14 ·

Her death was all Daddy's fault.

That was how he put it—to himself, to his friends, his colleagues, anyone who asked with the right note of deference, a respectful nod. He hadn't struck her down himself, he said. But he might as well have. If only he had understood more of his own heart, back in his salad days. If only he'd been wiser in his young middle age. Not that anyone was capable of understanding anything before it happened to him, much less after. Life can be a ball hit at you too fast. He for one had thought he'd owned the world, at forty—back in those heady years, back when he believed he could handle anything, success fit so easily, like a glove. Why shouldn't everything else crease around you that way? But let me tell you one thing, my friend, I've learned, although it's hard to admit it: If you find a pretty girl, even a pretty one you think might really care about you, there's no guarantee she'll be able to keep up with you, anymore than a butterfly can keep up with a Boeing.

He should have known better than to fall in so heedlessly that way, and marry such a sweet young debutante thing. For her part, she did nothing wrong at all except look up at him with those cornflower blue eyes and that sweet round face, holding her playbill up as if an autograph would let her die and go to heaven happy. Back then it was so different, you see, the Theater, it was the center of everything, and he'd been running high all right, a little too high, but then suddenly, looking down, he'd realized how good it would be to get back to something basic, something more like home. So there he was, in Atlanta, with those dewy blue eyes looking up at him—and that was that. There are times when you don't think about anything except the warm surface of something you want, that Georgia peach of a face, what a pillow all her black hair would make, and how you deserved it, after all the years of grueling work. But still it was his fault, all his damned fault, in the end. He should have known two souls as different as theirs wouldn't be able to unite. A little Baptist debutante, a hard-working man. He should have realized they'd end up strangers once the rice was thrown in the garbage.

At the top of the curving stairs at the big house, Sarah had frowned at me from underneath her helmet. Let's keep on listening, she nodded at me.

Daddy went on:

Have you ever stopped and looked across your own dining

room table, and it was as if you were both sitting in complete darkness, at the opposite ends of a whale?

But the children, they had come along, thank goodness, and so for a while things had been much better: he'd been able to get back to his work, and her sweet round face hadn't looked so spoiled, so disappointed. Only, of course, he hadn't known then about all the drinking. But that was his fault, too. He hadn't been around enough. He hadn't kept an eye on everything. Certain problems, though he hadn't known it then, had run in his wife's family. Later the doctor's best guess was that the booze had started before the second baby was born. But still, that wasn't her fault, in the end. Some things fly at you whether you're able to catch them or not. In the end, it wasn't Helen's fault she'd left the babies sleeping in their cribs and gone out into a rainy night for ice cream. It wasn't the truck driver's fault either, who'd only stayed in his lane, doing what he was supposed to do, his job, pushing the speed limit, earning money for his family, it wasn't his fault he didn't react quickly enough, hadn't seen at a distance what was coming. That man had to swallow what had happened to him, and live with it. Yes, this is her picture, we keep it out here, on the foyer table, in memory and out of respect, although her ashes are with her family, they had insisted—no, no, nothing at the beach house, my chickadees need a place where they can be free from all morbid things—yes, I'll have to take you out there someday—you know, their poor mother never liked it out there, even after I went to all the trouble of getting it back. But look, here's Jeanie now, isn't this wonderful, let's go out into the sunroom, you'll want to ask her about your next set of clubs. She's so generous about giving advice, and can steer you in the right direction.

Sarah let go of the banister and went into her room. I followed and leaned in her doorway and asked: Do you think all that melted chocolate ice cream they found in her lap, was it for her, or was it for us?

The golf cart was parked crookedly in the shed. Sarah's car was under the house. Paul hung back behind the dunes, lingering, watching the light move between pieces of sea glass. I washed my feet at the outdoor shower and went on up.

My sister was leaning against my father's empty wicker chair, her arms folded over her thin chest. Daddy and Mama were on the sofa, side by side, smiling, still breathing fast, recovering from their climb up the stairs. They bent over and ruffled the fur on the stomachs of the dogs, who were twisting like otters on their backs.

"You're home fast," I said to my sister.

"It's that ridiculous bird."

"How'd it turn out?"

"It didn't. It's upstairs again. Nobody was at the sanctuary. It was closed, if you can believe that. A closed sanctuary?"

"It is Saturday," Daddy allowed.

"Sarah." Mama smiled. "We do appreciate your trying, dear. We really do."

"The building's closed for three weeks. People make it so hard for other people to do anything nice. We should just push it off the balcony."

"Dear, the way it was sitting in its box, it didn't seem *ready.*"

"I think we're going to have to adopt it," my father put in.

Paul slid the door back.

"You there! Boy!" My father pointed.

He started. "Sir?"

"You called it right about this light today! Look! I'm going to appear positively golden in my study. I'm already as photogenic as a nectarine."

Paul narrowed his eyes, as though he were adjusting the level of glare in the room. "I think we should wait a little bit longer, sir."

"Son, I say we do it right after lunch. No sense wasting any more time. I have a few other things I have to tend to."

"Do you mind?" Sarah said. "*I'm* the director here."

"But I'm all ready," Daddy said plaintively. "We have to tell them, Jeanie, what a revved-up morning we've had."

"They're dying to tell us," I said. "Just look at their faces."

"It wasn't anything *all* that special, dear."

"She's underplaying it," Daddy said.

"Well, you can play whatever games you like." Sarah sat in his chair, taking it over. "But when I say shoot, we shoot."

"Then," Mama said, "we'd better talk quickly."

They had started out early because they wanted things still to look cool and fresh in the morning light, and to get their drive in before any other wanderers showed up on the beach. The only plan was to take the cart out farther than they had in a long, long time. That way, Mama explained it, they would know they hadn't missed any interesting things the last storm had washed in. While they were out they decided, why not, they would drive a few miles farther and see the old ship's boiler blown in by Allison—or had it been Alicia?—and see if it was still standing, half buried, a rusted snout pushing up through the sand. After that, they'd gone all the way out to Leak Lake, which was high after the rains, and drove in between the dunes and watched the trapped water ripple and turn pink while the sun rose higher and the bugs began swarming over in clouds. Mama then backed the cart out and they wound their way past a necklace of jellyfish that must have been traveling together and gotten too high during the storm. They'd lost their ticket, poor dears, and were done for. After a quick stop at the mini-mart, they headed back, and just past the corroded hood of the old defunct Ford, right where the grazing land started on the other side of the dunes, they saw what looked like a figure all by itself, dancing near the waves, making slow arm movements, the way the Chinese do tai chi, elbows stretching out.

Suddenly something had roared by the cart like an airplane.

"He was flying one of those kites with two strings, dears. They can do just about anything they want to these days."

Paul sat up excitedly. "A stealth kite!"

"A stunt kite, dear. Anyway, when we got closer," she went on, sitting back on the sofa, "that was when we saw he was really a surfer—at least, there was a board up by the dunes when we drove by, and a wetsuit next to it."

"He had to be more optimistic than most," my father said. "The waves were no higher than sheep's backs at that point. Did you mention he was naked?"

"I was just coming to that."

My father nodded. "And really something to look at. Moving back and forth from the water. Like a dancer. Like a little brown Nijinsky."

Mama said gently, "Let me finish, dear."

Now this boy, he was all smiles when they pulled up next to him and stopped and watched from a nice angle while he wove and darted the black wing of the kite, making it swoop and dive and spiral and curl and do things it didn't seem mere sticks and cloth could do.

"And there was a sound," Daddy said hushed. "Like skin flapping."

After a few minutes, the young man had shifted his position, moving back against the wind toward them, backing up until he was close enough to the cart that they could really see his face—such a boy, he was, that was all, he couldn't have been much over twenty—and now they understood why he was smiling and jerking his elbows toward them.

"I told your father he shouldn't, because of his heart."

"I told her she shouldn't because of her joints."

"But the wind was so strong up there."

"Yes, that was it. That was what made it so enticing."

So they'd done it: stripped their clothes off, their windbreakers, their nylon pants, their shoes, and joined him. "Only now I wish we hadn't kept anything on." Mama sighed and shook her head. "That *was* a little chicken of us, wasn't it?"

"But we embraced the *spirit* of the thing, Jeanie."

"Well, why didn't you?" Sarah asked pointedly. "Why didn't you go all the way?"

"We didn't want to steal his thunder," Daddy said.

"For a while we just watched him, to get the hang of it."

"It turns out this boy had already been all over the world, in his short life. Doing things like this—what he called X-sports. A born adventurer."

"He was tanned as smoked ham. You could hardly tell what he must have looked like when he started out."

"Skin cancer, anyone?" Sarah said.

"So I asked him," my father continued, "what made him so carefree? And he said, that he wasn't sure, but he thought maybe it had something to do with just trusting that the right things were always going to happen at the right time. He said that he never felt uncertain. Do you know"—he blinked—"I never really knew, until that moment, until that very moment, that in spite of everything I've tried, everything I've gone ahead and set up, I wasn't really such a wise parent. Because I hadn't made my children *ebullient.*"

My mouth hung open, along with Sarah's. What was that? An insult, an apology, or—?

"Then I thought, Now why does this boy seem so much *nicer* than my children?"

"Then he let us hold his kite."

She'd been the first one to try it, taking the padded handles while it still swooped in the air, and before she knew it she felt its power, its surge. "If only my wrists had been a little better, I could have done more maneuvers—but still, I was holding up to it, right up until it nose-dived, for *no* good reason, and popped me over on my face. But I kept on laughing and holding on, even with a mouthful of sand. Didn't I, Dee? And you couldn't wait. You wanted to take it from me before I was up on my feet again."

"It was like fighting a live thing."

"Yes." She seemed to hold her breath. "Like fishing in the air."

"I couldn't hold on to it for long, either."

"Well, dear, you haven't had a chance to work your upper-body strength recently."

And then, just like that, they had gotten it, they had understood: why the boy had to be, why you *had* to be naked, why that was, really, the only way to be matched to the thing, to be equal to it.

"Do you know, Jeanie, it's so strange? But for a minute I almost forgot—I almost forgot—"

"I know, dear," she nodded.

And then they had thanked the surfer, and waved goodbye to him, and gone back to the cart, hurriedly putting their slickers on, and then sitting there, for a while, just watching him. And then the last thing that had happened was that he had started back toward them, backing up again, keeping the kite in the air but edging toward them, feeling his way with his heels through the sand like a turtle pushing for the dunes, and then all of a sudden he'd winked, and brought the kite down low, and with a practiced jerk bent his knees and shot the lines up at the same time and followed them and jumped, jumped, jumped, so that he sailed, just like that, right off the ground, like a heron over the beach, and landed fifty feet away from them at the edge of the gray water.

"Well." My father suddenly let his breath out.

"Well," Mama said.

And now all the air in the room seemed to go slack. The cushions underneath them even seemed to lose their buoyancy.

"I ought to try and get some writing done," my father said, and he stood unsteadily, the pontoon of his stomach rocking him.

He worked his way around the wicker and toward the French doors.

He opened them, closed them, and rolled the bamboo shades down on the other side.

Mama stood and asked surprisingly, "You all make lunch? I want to take a little nap upstairs. You can make whatever you want."

"All right, Mama," Sarah also stood, tossing my father's clinging shawl aside. "Don't you worry about it. Go take a nice little rest. I've got everything all under control down here."

"Thank you, dear."

When she was near the top of the stairs, Paul excused himself hurriedly, too, and said he had to go on up to see about something.

"Well, that was interesting." I hoped Sarah would react.

She rolled her eyes and rubbed her wrists at the breaking points. "Let's make some sandwiches. The sooner we get a few things done around here, the sooner we can head on out. If we're lucky, maybe before another one of these ebullient escapades breaks out."

· 15 ·

When we were thirteen and fourteen, my father decided we were old enough to be in control of ourselves, and took us to rehearsals for any of his plays that passed through town, sometimes picking us up at school and telling us to forget homework and try to remember that childhood was a time for the unexpected.

There is a musk that clings to some theaters. A smell of dust and paint and velvet and fresh skin. There is the hush of thick padded doors. A sense of space, and yet intimacy, as though you've been invited into an internal organ. All that plush, overdone red. The sections of the house, divided by aisles, seemed to me like arteries. The proscenium arch was a hole in the back of a heart, and the stage itself was the hole behind the hole, its wings and backdrops exposed, its entrails, the ropes and wires and nerves of the lights.

The actors didn't interest me very much at first, they tended to be overdrawn, cartoonish at the start of things. The director and the producers were the centered, strong ones, by comparison, and my father, watching from the center row, his chin balanced on the tips of his fingers, his body leaning forward in his seat. They all leaned forward, poised, as if straining to hear something concealed under the actors' feet. What fixed my attention most was the slant of the house downward to the center of the stage with its brightness like lights at the end of a tunnel; the vertigo that pointed everything in one direction. I got that part, right away. What the theater was about. That it was about what you had to do to get people to sit still and stare into a hole.

Sarah usually got bored after the first hour.

"I'm going on down to Traps," she'd say.

I might take the service elevator down to check on her and find her wandering around under the ribs of the stage, the actors' feet still blundering muffled overhead, their voices muffled, too.

"It's like they're carrying their heads around in bags," I said once. "You shouldn't be down here alone."

"I want to show you something."

"What?"

"It's like this," she held her arms wide.

"What?"

"Don't be coy. I hate that." She dropped her arms and her shoulders sagged against a rolling metal prop crate. Her red hair fell forward over her face. She pushed against the crate. It didn't budge.

"You'll burst a gut," I said.

"It's like being underground. This same, low pounding. And a light, like this, that goes out." She reached and tried to tap one of the caged bulbs. "Then *pfft.* Then nothing."

She'd never told me this much about her seizures before. Not that I would have dared ask.

"All right, I get it."

"No you don't. You can't."

"Then why are you telling me?"

"Because people shouldn't go around thinking they don't know something because they haven't asked to find out what they don't know. Where're you going?"

"To the Green Room to get a Coke. Come on, you're not staying down here alone. Mama would kill me."

"I'll be glad if you get a car." She moved away from the heavy crate. "We can start seeing less of each other."

That Christmas, one of her gifts was a new cashmere sweater, and one of mine was a new suede coat. Mama making sure everything was fair and square. Daddy had barely been out of his office all day, working intensely. But that evening he came down and we all sat in the comfortable leather armchairs in the sitting room. Except for Sarah, who stayed on the floor.

"How peaceful it is down here," Daddy said.

"Christmas is becoming too frantic, isn't it?" Mama nodded. "People running in and out of stores like they're trying to save everything from a fire." She leaned back in her chair, and the firelight caught her square chin as it turned from one to the other of us, lingering each time. And I remember thinking, Maybe love has to be balanced, that way. Evenly. Carefully measured. Because otherwise it was an elephant left on a seesaw. Embarrassing, ridiculous, unless you sat an elephant on the other side.

Outside the street was gray, and getting darker, and the wind was whistling, tossing up the bags of mistletoe against the windows. Inside the fire crackled behind its screen. All the gift wrap was already contracted and melted inside it.

"Well," Daddy said restlessly. "I have to be on my way."

Sarah looked up from the rug.

"It's a new project, chickadee. Someone special's in town with his investor's pockets, and only tonight, to see some of his family."

"Dee, you take a muffler. It's bad out."

"This is *Christmas,*" Sarah said.

"Are my gloves in the hallway?"

"Ars longa, vita brevis," I told her.

"Oh, you two," Mama teased us. "I can see it all again, you're six years old and miserable. But you have to understand, dears. Anything you really want to stay on top of, you have to stay on top of."

"I'll be back as soon as I can, Jeanie."

"We're not waiting up," Sarah said.

He looked down at her, patiently. "Sometimes you don't get a second chance to make something happen. Something difficult and worthwhile and untried—You'll see for yourself one day."

"Daddy," I decided to try. "Come on."

He stopped and looked at me. For a moment I thought he took

the room in, really took it in, saw the fire leaping up, and the fingers of the Christmas tree reaching out, and the glints of ribbon left on the floor—but then whatever it was inside him started to come over him, the thing that pulled him away.

"This is how our mother ended up dead you know," Sarah said.

He looked back at Mama for a long moment, and then turned on his heel and left the room.

From my bedroom window I saw my sister stalking down the street, nothing covering her but her thin, new sweater. Her flying hair looked electric under the lamps.

I went into her room. She'd left a note on her round desk. The furniture in her room was round as a precaution.

I'm leaving. Forever. This is INSUFFERABLE. And next to this, for effect, she'd left the bottles filled with her anti-seizure medications.

I opened each one of them and took some of the pills out and stuck them in my jeans. Then I took out another piece of her pink stationery and rewrote the note. *We're leaving. This is insufferable. Forever.*

By the end of the block I was so cold I was biting my hands. On the next block, halfway down, a house was being torn down and its new incarnation rising from inside it. The bricks were going up, but the windows weren't in yet. I saw a shadow flitting inside. And this was the thing about Sarah. She didn't have to go far to make a point.

I found her in one of the gutted rooms in the back, out of the wind, hunched down by a sawhorse, her knees pulled up to her chest like pincers.

"What's up, Sar?"

"What's up with you?"

"Mind if I join you?"

"Do."

It was one of those rare Decembers that was cold enough to make you think the geese had gotten mean and dragged winter farther south than usual.

"I brought you some of your pills."

"I don't need them." She held out her hand. "I already have some."

"I have to admit I like your style. Maybe I'll take them?"

What would happen, I'd always wondered? Would I get stoned beyond caring? Beyond forgetting that I'd never get the boy in my poli sci class into the school bathroom? Would I throw up? Would I fall asleep? Would the drugs reverse in my system, turning negative, and instead of keeping me conscious, shock me into fits?

"Don't be stupid." She grabbed them quickly. "You'll hurt yourself."

We sat next to each other, leaning against the stripped wall but not touching. We worked our way around to talking about patricide. A film, about Lizzie Borden, had been on television that week. The actress's performance was overstated, yes, but what about the action itself? There was a lot to recommend it. Sarah approved especially of the movie's theory about how Lizzie got rid of the weapon, dropping it down into a latrine. We could use our father's gun, and then lower it into some convenient smelter. When we'd had enough of this we regressed to childhood and practiced making one leg longer than the other and then healing it. We listed the foods that were the most disgusting to us. We made up limericks:

There once was a girl from Lubbock
Who hated to sleep on her stomach

It was the dead of night by then, so we stood, and ducked under the strips of hanging sheet plastic, and hid down in the front of the house, by one of the windows, and watched while they drove, in their separate cars, up and down the street, up and down, up and down, looking for us, craning, windows rolled low to the iciness. For another hour or so we shivered and watched them circling around us.

"It almost makes you feel sorry," I said.

"Almost," Sarah said.

It was after one in the morning before we finally admitted our toes felt like lead pipe, and got up and started the one block home. Our plan was simply to saunter up the circular drive and in through the front door, with no explanation. But the freezing weather must have gotten to us. Our excitement must have given us away, the crunch of our feet on the gravel, our silhouettes flashing in front of the windows. Because as we opened the door, there they were, in the sitting room, exactly as if nothing had happened, exactly as if they'd had time to arrange themselves, picking up one of their reviews or *Sports Illustrateds* lying around on the tables. My father looked up, feigning surprise. "Chickadees? Been out late to see the decorations?"

Sarah said nothing, heading for the stairs. I didn't move. I was fixed on Mama's face. She was calm, settled, as she turned her pages. When her gray eyes did turn and rest on mine, she held me for so long, so steadily, for such a long minute, I felt my toes stinging and melting. And I understood what she was saying to me. Did you really think you would beat *me* playing such a cheap game, dear? Did you, now?

· 16 ·

I told Sarah I was going upstairs to take a nap.

"No lunch?" She spread her hands out over the crawfish sandwiches we'd just made. "No carbo-loading for the rest of the weekend?"

"I didn't sleep all that much last night. Besides, I'm all worn out over the idea of that naked kite flier."

"You do need a boyfriend."

Up in my room again, I stared down at the white, stapled pages Paul had left on my pillow.

What if I just took your little play outside, Mr. Vanek, and went downstairs, and dropped it in the trash bin with all the crawfish tails? What if I buried it somewhere behind the dunes, and let it slowly rot? Are you aware of your total lack of what we writers like to call *a sense of timing?*

Not five feet away I could hear him pacing on the other side of the thin wall, shaking the floor between us, excitedly, bobbing it like a diving platform. After a while apparently he couldn't take it anymore; from behind my closed door I heard the sound of his sandals pocking down the stairs. When Sarah called out it was time for lunch, I kept reading, and didn't move from my bed.

Jean Dugan, Mama, once told me she sympathized with my father and me—but that it was hard to see how we got any *satisfaction* out of the work we did, when there was really so little *to* it. There was nothing, really, like actually doing something. Pulling your arms back and feeling the weight of your shoulders swinging from the hook of your neck. Trusting your knees to make good on a long bet placed by your eyes. Aiming for a target that changed every single time you faced it—nothing compared to it, dears, nothing even came close.

My father tried arguing that this sounded exactly like what he did, every day, but she only laughed at him, and shook her head, and pointed to her bag of clubs leaning on its stand in the hallway. No, dear, what an artist does is something other people might be able to do, but they can't think of it. But what we sportsmen excel at are things other people can think of, but just can't do.

If you went out with her on the course (and Sarah and I had been allowed to ride in the cart when we were old enough), you saw she was relaxed and jokey, talking and walking with her partners nonchalantly up the fairway, but that her eyes were always on the horizon. If you asked her she would say, no, she hadn't exactly been born to the game, but had been lucky enough to fall into it. In the Carolinas, everybody was mad about something outdoorsy and sporting and green, and lucky for her, her adoptive parents had been turf people, incredibly active, they'd scooped her up out of an orphanage she couldn't even remember being dropped at by whoever left her there. Times were so hard, back then, but only imagine, these folks had come along and wanting to help out, just stepped right in, older people with no children of their own, and took in a strange, hungry toddler. There had been a warm house to grow up in, and lessons, and school, and good manners to learn, and trips to the horse races. But most of all on long Saturdays, the links, shooting and putting, putting and shooting—anything worth doing, her father said, was worth doing a lot of to do well. By the time she was fifteen she'd beaten every boy at the local athletic club. She was just about to go off to college when her mother died, and then, soon after, her father—they were well into their eighties by then, you have to remember, and you know how old married people are about sticking together. No, they didn't live to see her develop, to see how she eventually turned out.

There was no trick to winning, she said, only the moment when after you'd mustered all your skill and concentration, you had the chance to be decisive, to understand where you stood, and that you had it in your power to do something about it. There was no trick except understanding that nothing stood between you and the top of a mountain but a short piece of grass that looked deceptively flat. To really see it, you had to lie down in it, in your mind's eye, and feel its every turn and contour, until you knew exactly what was necessary, no more and no less, and measured it out. And then you stood up. And fixed your grip. And made sure everything pointed toward the hole, every millimeter of muscle and mettle. Because the hole, in that moment, was all. And then . . . Some things just can't be put into words, dears. Winning isn't like anything else at all.

Downstairs the three of them were crowded into my father's study. Daddy was busy sorting his yellow notepads on his desk, and throwing a few balls of wadded paper into the trash can. Paul was adjusting the shades over the windows to get the light he wanted. The camera was up on its tripod. I smiled at all of them. Gloriously. I smiled gloriously from my towering height at poor Paul, poor, naïve, clumsy, beaten Paul.

But I gave him a little credit. He was right about the light. It was divine. My father's study was glowing like a gourd lit from the inside.

Sarah was getting him settled with a professionalism I wouldn't have expected, positioning him in his chair.

"And please don't fuss with that mike anymore, Daddy."

"It's itching."

"That's your imagination. There's nothing on you to scratch."

I was still smiling gloriously, giving nothing away to Paul. "Have I missed anything? Where's Mama?"

"She went to lie down again after lunch." My sister fussed with my father's collar. "She said she's seen all this before. Harry, will you move that pile of magazines out of frame for me? Daddy, do you need a bottle of water or anything while we shoot?"

"No." He grimaced, and dropped his chin on his chest, looking askance. The dogs lay obediently in the corner, their heads on their paws.

"Where is the bird again?" he fretted.

"Please don't get started, Daddy."

"She won't let me have him in the frame." He flicked his eyes at me. "She doesn't want me to look like one of those people who take in strays. Certain odd behaviors are implied. Obsessions. Odors."

Sarah stepped back, a pleased look on her face. "Your hair looks just right like that, Daddy. All puffed."

My father had shaved; the outline of his jaw was so sharp, it looked like it would cut through the skin.

"Are we ready?" he said impatiently.

"Sir, almost." Paul had been staring at me, but now he hopped to it, coming to, and held the light meter again to my father's chest.

"All right." Sarah took a breath in. "So let's review. All we really need to cover now is some of the material going back to the thirties and forties, and then I want you to talk for a while about how you feel about the body of your work, since it's something you can envision, finally, in its entirety. Then later while the sun's going down we can get some nice shots of the house and of you walking around on the beach."

"Envision it in its entirety?"

"Any problem with that, Daddy?"

"It doesn't sound fun."

"It's not supposed to be fun. It's supposed to be revealing. Are you relaxed? Are you comfortable?"

Paul peered through the camera's lens. "This is really good."

My father blinked at Sarah, who was taking her place now, professionally, behind Paul. He looked at Paul; at the dogs lying down in the corner; at me off to one side; and then back again at Sarah. Trapped.

"Are we rolling?"

"Yes, sir."

"Okay, Daddy. Why don't you tell us a little bit about what it felt like after Doris and Patrick died."

Suddenly he nodded, relaxing, growing . . . sage.

"It was like falling down with Alice's rabbit. Things were never the same again, truthfully. Our family all but fell to rack and ruin, the day that fishing pier went down. We might never have recovered, except I was sent to live with some cousins, out in Hempstead, and they took me in, grudgingly. Hard times, hard times, in those days. It was rough for people to take in even one more hungry child to feed."

Paul gave a thumbs-up. Sarah nodded at my father.

"But how did you *feel* after your parents died?"

"How did I *feel?*"

"Respond, emotionally, as a twelve-year-old boy?"

He rubbed his elbow. "I'm not sure I remember. I do remember understanding we were just one of thousands, in trouble. People were hanging themselves, in some cases. Dying of typhoid. Abandoning their homes. I know I felt bad. Very, very bad."

"What do you remember about your parents?"

"That they were good, decent people. They did what they could for as long as they could. My father could make a toy, a game, out of anything. My mother was a talker and loved to tell stories. She was a loquacious woman."

"We can intercut the pictures here," she said to Paul. "How was life at the cousins'?"

"Drudgery. Hard work. The older boy and I, one summer, we found two rusted almost impossible scythes in a ditch, and spent a week scraping and resharpening them. Then we went out and offered to cut down anything people would let us cut down. We worked for about a dollar a day. A dollar a day. Imagine that. That kind of money, in those days— It was high cotton, let me tell you. We worked from dawn till dusk, the two of us."

"But then you ran away from his house?"

"I didn't say I was enjoying his company."

Daddy rode the rails and in the backs of trucks. Up and down the state, there was still enough cotton to pick and enough people who somehow weren't affected by the general downturn in things, and could pay not to pick it themselves. The work was nasty, brutish, but he was glad enough to get it when he could. He would work with anyone, of course. You didn't bother with things like color. People simply found ways to come together. Not because human beings were any better, back then, God knows they weren't, and the bodies still showed up lynched in the trees. But out in the rows all you could hope was that whoever was picking next to you would have the decency to put a gin bag over your face if you happened to drop with sunstroke. The world was the same as it always was, charity and self-interest, self-interest and charity, side by side. And in some camps the walls were no thicker than a soapbox.

"I can remember, with perfect clarity, the day that man from the WPA drove in and wanted to take pictures of all of us. I was never one to pass up a chance at doing something for money, and I made myself useful by going around and writing down the names of all the people he was taking pictures of who couldn't write themselves, with descriptions of what they were wearing and what they'd said, so he could match the material up later. Basically I made myself into an assistant on the spot. He wanted to know how I'd gotten to be so sharp, and I told him about the books and Mother teaching me at home, and the next thing I knew he was offering me a ride out West. I got work right off in Los Angeles as a gofer in a publicity department, which meant that by the time the war broke out I was in good shape, writing ad copy and in '43 assigned to propaganda and radio plays. It kept me from being sent over—which I only half liked, but it was fabulous training, even if I already understood radio wasn't where the action was. And the rest, as they say, is mastery."

"Good voice-over stuff. So now, Daddy, tell me why, even though some of your work is set during that time, you never wrote any plays about yourself. Tell us why you've written about seemingly every other kind of person you've met, but not about an orphan picking cotton to get to California?"

"I thought that was obvious, chickadee. I'm not so self-absorbed."

· 17 ·

"Shakespeare!" Paul looked up from his eyepiece, excitedly. "He didn't write about himself either!"

"Let's try a different setup, now," Sarah directed. "Let's experiment with a different angle."

It took Paul a few minutes to adjust the shot. The light in the room had shifted. A ridge of clouds had moved in from the west and was hovering just over the rigs in the distance.

Paul seemed impatient with his equipment, now, awkward, as if tied to the camera, his ball and chain. My father waited patiently, looking out at the haze, resting an arm on top of one of his blank notepads. He always left the first page of his notes empty.

Underneath were his scribbles and diagrams and half-worked-out scenes. The blank sheet, he said, was to remind you of where you had started.

"All set again, sweetheart? All right. Now, Daddy, why don't you go ahead and sum up your work for us. Give us a kind of rundown."

"Like a grocery list?"

"Come on, Dad. So how do you feel about having written all of those plays? Winning all of those awards? The whole thing?"

He tilted his long head to one side, the pale folds of skin at his neck compressing. "I think I'm still just doing the best I can, for as long as I can. I think that's really all there is to it, in the end. Consistency. Determination. Spunk. You have to stick with something, I believe. You have to *cleave* to it, and not flit and flutter around from this to that but really hold on to something, something difficult, until the very end, until you know you're done with it, and it's done with you."

"Is that supposed to mean something, Daddy?"

"What?" he blinked.

"You know I can edit that out. I can edit out anything I want to."

"What, daughter? Was that part unclear?"

"Oh, it was clear enough, Daddy. I know what you're saying to me. But what if I put it to you this way: How is it really 'sticking' with anything, in the end, writing one play, and then going off, and writing another? Aren't you always, in a sense, leaving things behind? Ideas? People? Floating off? Don't you, in a way, use the people in your plays, for a while, and then give them up, forget about them, and go on? I'm just curious how would you respond if I put the question to you that way?"

He pondered, bewildered, frowning, his eyebrows twitching while he stared down at the blank sheet on his pad. "No! No. That's not it. You don't leave them. I wouldn't say that, no. They come to *you,* first, for one thing. It's very strange how it happens. They're like ghosts, in the beginning. But ghosts that haven't lived, or even been born yet. Which means you have to work backwards in the process, looking for clues about them, about who they might have been, from the way they haunt you. And it's because of this, this *listening,* and trying to pay attention, always going backwards, backwards, that you never really get away from them, and they never leave you. I think people who don't understand this"—he fidgeted suddenly, straightening—"can't really be blamed for it. It's not for everyone, this line of work. But it's all right." He smiled and waved a relieved hand at the camera, in our directions. "Luckily, there are secondary forms."

"And there you have it," Sarah turned to me. "We're secondary forms."

"That's not what I'm saying at all, chickadee."

"Oh, Daddy. I think you are."

I hadn't noticed how the light in the room had gone gray. The sound of the surf had changed. It was low, hissing now. I looked past the camera, out the windows, and saw all those white backs rearing.

My sister looked tired, the white streak in her hair taking on the gray in my father's study.

"Come on, sweetie," Paul looked at her, nervously. "It's not so good, this part."

My father was sitting up straight in his chair. I could see the veins rippling in his neck. Be careful, Sar. A man-o'-war washed up on the beach.

"So, chickadees, are we done now?"

"Not just yet, Daddy."

"I'm a little tired."

"I said we're not finished, Daddy?"

"A little hint, daughter? Subjects don't respond well to coercion?"

"Can't *stick with it,* Daddy?"

He leaned forward, casual, as if listening for something, footsteps outside the door. But there was no way Mama could hear any of this. "Come on, now," he objected. "I raised you all to have better manners."

"You didn't raise us at all, Daddy. I guess you don't want that recorded, though. That you let a poor sick drunk woman try."

He flinched. "I see. So that's what this is all about. Well, are you satisfied with yourself, now? Have you gotten everything you wanted?"

"No. I'm not satisfied."

"Then that makes two of us." He pointed at the camera, toward Paul. "But no point in getting crabby. It's time to turn this thing off."

"Sweetheart," Sarah said calmly. "Don't you move."

"Sarah—" I stepped forward.

"No?" Paul asked.

"Don't you move." She turned to him. "Don't you move one little hair on your sweet head."

He didn't know what to do. Paul. He looked at my father. He looked at me, for some clue. He blinked again at Sarah. He shifted his weight from one foot to the other. My father adjusted, too, in his rolling chair, but kept his face serene, saintly, even going for the pitiable. "So what's the plan? Am I being taken hostage? Will you refuse to feed me, unless I submit? Are you trying to break my poor, weak, tired heart?"

"Give it up, Daddy. I never saw a redder herring."

"Turn it off," I said decisively to Paul.

"You are so full of it, Daddy, do you know that? So full of shit. And never more than when you think you're being honest."

The look on his face was terrible. Then suddenly his face flattened, and his eyes went down and deep. I could hear his controlled, labored breathing.

"Enough. You're going to hurt your brain, dear, with all this stress. I just wish you'd allow for your poor, erratic brain."

"That's how you've always secretly thought of it, isn't it?"

"Don't get overblown. I know it's been a burden to you. We all have our burdens." He looked from one to the other of us. "We all end up having to live with our disappointments, chickadees."

"Was that why you always found it so hard to live with us, Daddy?"

"I never said that, daughter."

She pointed at the camera. "You just did Daddy. And I've got it now, on the record. Never let anyone have the last word. Isn't that what you used to say? Especially about what is clearest to you. Never give that up, not even when you've been backed into a corner."

"Is . . . is that what this is?" he said, paling.

"For God's sake, turn it off!" I lunged for the camera.

I felt Paul tackling me, of all things. We were actually fighting, each of us trying to pull the other's hand off the slippery lens. His eyes were bulging, stressed, shot through with yellow up close to mine, but not looking at me, so pained, straining over toward my father, he looked to him hungrily, longingly, torn, the whites of his eyes shaking until I thought they would burst, he was so poised between his two ideas, his two ambitions. And then I felt him give toward my father, go in that direction, and I knew, even if Sarah didn't know it yet, I knew exactly what was going to happen next. I knew who Paul was going to choose, what the most seductive thing in the room was, always winning out, secure, no matter how you tried to get ahead of it.

Paul held me in a kind of headlock; for a minute, we didn't move. Nothing happened. Everything was so still. I could hear the dogs growling low in their throats. Then I felt Paul let go of me.

I fell to the floor.

"Sweetheart," he turned to her, "do you want me to turn the camera off now?"

"All right, sweetie." She nodded. "Off."

He reached for the side of the camera, and after this quick switch, they locked eyes, privately, forgiving each other.

I watched them. Amazed.

My father turned white.

"Get out," he exhaled, the words so low they were hardly words. "Get out now, please." The dogs were up with their tails wagging excitedly.

"Get *out!*"

"Daddy." I stood and reached for him. "It's okay. It's all right now."

"What? Who's this? Oh. Noises from the peanut gallery."

I turned and grabbed Sarah by the arm. "Let's go."

· *18* ·

They were throwing their things into their backpacks. I caught Paul sliding the pages of his play—I'd left it in his closet—discreetly under his swim trunks.

"Wait," Sarah said, matter-of-fact. "I need to get our stuff out of the bathroom."

When she was gone, I pointed.

"I did read it. I want you to know. Every word."

"Thank you, Harry. Bad timing today, though. I'm so sorry."

"That wasn't your fault. That bit, down there."

"It's so hard, sometimes."

"Don't worry about it, Paul."

The house was ringing, but with a stranger hum than usual.

"Anyway." I touched his arm. "You've made a good start, haven't you?"

"I have?"

"Well, actually, no. It was awful. But don't get me wrong about that. Everyone's awful, in the beginning."

"Okay . . ." He nodded after a moment, accepting this.

"So . . . were the actors dressed up—like sharks—supposed to be . . . Communists?"

"They were supposed to be Death."

"Right. Well. There are always revisions."

Sarah came back and tossed in her shampoos and color conditioners.

"That's it," she said.

"You're just taking off, then, Sar? Just like that? And I'm left holding the bag?"

"So don't stay, Harry. It's enough. Haven't you had enough for one weekend?"

"My flight isn't until Monday."

"Change it then. It's your life."

"You're not—" I pointed down at the video. "You're not really going to use any of that?"

"Harry"—she turned on me suddenly—"why are you always so protective? What on earth are you *thinking?* That one day, if you put some blockbuster up on the stage, he's going to stand up and cheer and go all blubbery and cover you with roses and kisses? It won't be like that. You know that. Even if he had eighty more years. It all has to be him."

"I'm just trying to be fair."

"Well, then grab one of those, would you?" She pointed at the bags. "God, Har. Don't make us do *everything.*"

Downstairs everything was deserted. Willie and Able had even carried their chew toys away. We slid the door closed behind us and went down under the house and started loading the bags into the car's trunk. It was getting so dark already. Every day shorter than the last one.

Paul shook my hand, warmly. "You should come and see us?" Then he tactfully got into the driver's side and shut the door.

"Okay, then," I said to Sarah.

"You do understand, right?" She brushed something imaginary off my shoulder. "You do know I just wanted him to feel it, for once?"

"So it's enough now."

"I don't know. It depends on how I feel later . . ."

The joists under the house were humming. She turned and bent and checked on Paul through the rear window.

"I don't know how he puts up with all of this," she sighed. "And he doesn't even know the half of it."

"That's probably a good thing."

"I'm afraid," she said, half laughing, but half shivering, "he thinks I'm bizarre enough as it is."

"He cares about you. Trust me on that."

"He's patient."

"You're lucky."

"Do you know"—she jerked her head toward the upstairs—"I

think they sometimes think the whole world is still watching them? It's crazy. This idea that anybody cares, that anyone *would* care, even give a hoot. Woody runs off with Soon-Yi. Nobody minds. But you know what, Harry? It's all passing them by now. The phone never rings at all anymore. No one is paying attention. They're outliving every interesting thing they've ever done."

"You better go now."

"As long as you're all right. You sure you're all right?"

"I'm fine."

"Say goodbye to Mama for us when she wakes up. Who knows, she'll probably be glad we're out of here."

"Be careful driving."

"We will." She smiled, mischievously, like a girl. "I've got so many things to do, you know, to pull together. So many projects to get off the ground. I'm starting a piece about this great new country band, and I've got this romantic short I'm shopping around, and then there's the work on Daddy's thing still to polish up, and I've got some other great ideas. . . . I've got to get back into the thick of things." So much, I thought, for that twelve-year-old girl or boy in the former Yugoslavia. She reached for the door handle. "So many things to shoot. But then, it's no problem. I'm a multitasker."

· 19 ·

We always met at the big house on the Fourth of July, because it was generally a slow time of year for all of us, and Mama could persuade us to come down from our colleges and eat all the salt ham and pork-and-beans and slaw and corn bread she could make, and keep the sparklers from catching my father's eyebrows on fire.

The year I finished graduate school, I decided to out myself to them officially. I was twenty-five years old, and things were getting ludicrous. If it walks like a duck, quacks like a duck. . . . I didn't prepare much of a scene—how does a duck surprise a family of ostriches?—but I did plan on being relaxed, casual. Offhand.

At the big house there was a rental car parked in the circular driveway—Sarah must have paid somebody to drop her off, was all I thought at the time.

The shades were still down in the front of the house. I found my family out back, in the air-conditioned sunroom, sitting around the glassy garden table.

"What took you so long?" Sarah asked. "Your plane was here two hours ago."

"Slow at the rental counter. I hit some traffic. Any special hurry?"

"Dear." Mama smiled, folding her hands. "How does it feel to be done with school? We're so proud of you. And so glad to see you."

Sarah interrupted. "Mama's just stalling. They had a car accident last night. That's their rental, out there."

"What—what kind of accident?"

"Sit down, dear, and let's not get ahead of ourselves."

"But why didn't somebody call me, before I left?"

"We didn't want you to get all worried, dear, about something that was already over and done with. We didn't see the point to it." She lifted the muscled flaps of her arms from the table, and sank them back down. I saw cuts on her elbows. "Besides, we didn't want you to be distracted, any risk to yourself while you were driving in from the airport."

"Look at Daddy, Har. *He's* in deep sauce."

My father's hair was a little flat on one side. His cut fingers traced the surface of the glass table, drumming it.

"It was a close call," he said.

Together they passed the cold coal of the story back and forth between them.

The night before, late, as they were coming home from a dinner party downtown, it had started to rain. The potholes had filled, as usual, and the streets had turned black and slick and mucky as tar, but Mama had simply slowed down, working her way through the theater district, staying clear of the freeway, and at one point having to follow a detour because of some roadwork. That was why they ended up getting lost for a while, down near the edge of one of the wards, next to the feeder road. They were fine, though, just going along beside the highway, when all of a sudden they heard something deafening bearing down on them from the off-ramp. It was a truck with a huge tanker behind it. Sparks were showering from its sides and underneath it, and all she could do was veer sharply to one side and let it roar honking past. Ahead at the intersection, straight in front of them, it broadsided a car coming from the right. It ran over a pair of people in the lighted crosswalk, and then everything stopped, in a horrible tangle, at a brick retaining wall just past a late-night market. And then it all burst into flames.

They had watched, horrified, still butted up against the right curb. A pickup truck coming from behind them must not have seen them, the driver must have been overwhelmed at the sight of the fireball in front of them. The pickup truck's brakes hit so hard it skidded and flipped over and landed half on top of them. It all happened so fast they had no time to react. They were pinned, before they knew it, and sunk down low into their seats behind the crushed butterfly of the windshield. For a long time they couldn't see anything, only hear. They talked to each other, determining that, as far as they could tell, they were both in one piece. They waited, listening to the screeching and the sirens. Eventually they heard the Jaws of Life; it took two hours to cut them out. By that time the tanker and the car and the people fused inside it had been doused with foam.

"We were able to walk away." My father shook his head slowly. "It was sheer luck. They took us past the news cameras and got us into an ambulance together. Even the paramedics couldn't believe it, checking us out. We had nothing more than scratches on us."

Mama turned. "That's when we overheard one of the policemen saying they might have to use the DNA procedures, because those bodies would be so badly burned, and . . ."

For a moment, none of us was able to say anything. The room seemed small, as though the windows had sunk a foot lower into the ground.

"But you did go to the hospital?" I spoke up quietly. "You did have yourselves completely checked out?"

"Yes, dear, of course," Mama said. "They sent us home this morning."

"You know"—he turned and looked straight at me—"your life doesn't flash in front of your eyes, son. It just balls up."

My sister was looking at them, curiously. "No. There's something more. I don't know what it is. But there's something more."

"We do have to get things straight." He turned to Mama.

"Yes. We could have been—" Mama stopped. "We were almost— And then, autopsies, reports, filings, who knows, Harry and Sarah could have been told something confusing, something they wouldn't know how to handle, something that wouldn't be fair to them. It was our mistake, Dee. We never thought this sort of thing through, at the beginning."

"Things happen," my father said bracingly, facing the two of us. "Things can run together, rush into each other. Even if you don't mean for them to."

"Sarah. Harry. Dears. It's who I am. I was shipped off from Texas to North Carolina. I was only three years old."

"Our cousin Jeanie was sent to, out there, died of typhus. We somehow got word out in Hempstead that she did, too. There was no reason not to believe it. Times were so terrible, then. You swallowed everything you lost, and we all lost so much. You went on."

"The Dugans took me in from the orphanage. They changed my name. That was their idea, their way of helping me start over. I was so small, I couldn't know, couldn't finally remember anything about my family. But you don't forget your name. Even if you're just a little girl. You don't lose a thing like that."

"We put two and two together, after a while."

"After it was too late."

Their squared jaws had lined up perfectly next to each other on the other side of the table. But I'd always thought married couples, married couples—my mind was whirling, my eyes suddenly focusing as if I'd never tried before—that they always ended up looking—

"It knocked us flat," he said. "For a little while."

"You see, dears. We were already so much . . . so much . . ."

"So we decided it didn't matter. We were both past wanting more children, for one thing. And it was absolutely nobody's business but our own. So we stuck to it."

I felt for my own jaw. Catching it.

Sarah's eyes were bugging out.

"This is awkward, chickadees, I know. But it can't go beyond the four of us," my father said. "It's a complicated affair, to say the least, and there are all sorts of implications, legal and otherwise. You do understand, chickadees? You do understand what, what we're saying to you?"

My sister turned slowly, amazed, toward me. I saw her eyes run up and down my sibling body. Recoiling from me. *No.*

But she said, controlling her voice, "What's not to understand? Why should it even matter to us? Things like this are always happening on television— It's your own business anyway. It's no skin off our noses, in the end."

"Well, in a manner of speaking, it is, chickadee."

"What Sarah means is, it doesn't really change anything, does it?" I heard my voice squeaking. "I don't see how it does." And watching their reactions, saw it was true. They were sitting there, contented. They were still composed—if anything, more steady than they had been before. They hadn't wavered, hadn't faltered or even reached out to touch each other.

"Harry's exactly right." My step-mother-aunt smiled, relaxed. "Nothing has changed, not a wee bit. I'm *so* glad you see it that way, dears." She nodded, still without moving, keeping her strong, square hands folded. And I realized: This was it, then. This was why they'd always been so careful never to embrace in front of us. Because they were flesh and blood. Because giving something away about being flesh and blood, to flesh and blood, would be giving away too much. "We were so concerned that one of you might feel . . . upset."

What I felt was tired. Deflated. And . . . cheated.

"I guess it's almost dull by comparison." I straightened and heard myself almost pouting. "Me letting out that I'm gay, and all."

"God, Harry." Sarah shook her head. "Now?"

"It's funny, isn't it—but it's a little bit like being in the same boat," I went on, determined.

"Well . . ." My father hesitated. Mama seemed to be considering.

"Well, no, I wouldn't say it's the same," he finished.

"Dee?"

Sarah interrupted them again. "I think I may need a minute. I'm going upstairs. I feel just a little bit dizzy. Mama, you better come and monitor me on the way up."

Something tense was left in the room, something large and breathless and pounding, when they were gone.

"Not the same in any way at all, Daddy?"

He shifted in his chair across from me. "Well, you know, your mama and I . . ." He tried a laughing note. "Generally speaking, you know, we're still in the main . . . in the main tent."

"Do you know about how ridiculous that sounds?"

"There's no reason to call names, is there?" He acted hurt. "You can see for my part I am totally accepting of your news—and of you, son. Totally."

"Daddy. Come on. You never have been."

"You're the one being ridiculous now," he pointed out. "You know who I am, Harry. What I do for a living. The range of people I work with, and I'm friends with."

"You're disappointed, Daddy. It's all right. I've always known that. I've always seen it in your face. But why? I'm just curious—that's all."

He shifted again, leaning on the openwork arm of the sunroom chair. "I don't know if *disappointment* is the right word. Set back, maybe? I don't know. It must be a bit of ego. That's what I think it is, at least. But you can't really blame a father for that, son. You can't blame him, for wishing, for wanting his son to grow up to be like him, in some ways, at least, some important ways, to go on, like him, and have children, for one thing, and, and—"

"Gays and lesbians have children all the time."

"You want to preserve," he went on, not hearing this, "*yourself,* in some sort of fundamental, egotistical way. To continue. But don't you bother your head about any of that now, son. I'm not upset and I'm not worried at all. I promise you. It's your choice, and you'll be fine, you'll be just fine, if you take care of yourself, and keep your ear to the ground, and in the end, you know how Jeanie and I feel about this now, about life, that, that—obviously—we regard it as everyone's intimate arrangement."

"I'm still confused, though, about what you mean, 'in some fundamental way'?"

"What?"

"Being like you?"

His face had closed like a book.

The waves were pummeling one another, rolling over and over in the darkness. Sarah and Paul's taillights had long ago disappeared down the shelled road and into the mist. I turned away from my walk through the eddies and started toward the humps of the dunes again. The stars were splattered in the sky. All along the beach, the staggered houses were either lit by a single hooded lamp or left in dark outline. Except for our house. Its lights were on, both upstairs and down. The mist made the glowing windows seem blurry, more distant than they were. Hushed, and hushing. But then eyes are connected to ears, dear. One foot after the other, that's how you keep the ground underneath you.

· 20 ·

The Booby was shrieking through the air of the living room. I ducked under it. Mama swore. It was careening, wildly, flapping off a wall. The dogs were halfway up the furniture, after it. Mama shouted it would kill itself against the patio glass. I closed the door and threw my arms up defensively and the bird veered over the sofa, where it crashed, stunned, sinking down to the wicker back, its brown wings pinned against the paneled wall, its chest pressed up to the bullets in the wood, one foot flopping uselessly underneath it.

Mama took a breath and grabbed Willie, who was baring his teeth and getting ready to pounce. I got Able's front claws out of the cushions, and without a word to each other we darted around the corner and dumped them in the bathroom, Mama slamming the door while their nails were still scraping the porcelain, scrambling to get out.

She was out of breath, bending over, one hand braced on her knee.

"Shame on them." She coughed down through the floorboards. "Will you— *Shame* on them."

"It's all right, Mama. Let's go in and see. I don't think he's any worse off than he was before."

"Go on ahead, then."

The Booby was still splayed over the sofa, its neck craning around, showing fixed, panicked eyes.

"They went straight for his box." She came in behind me now, still breathing hard. "I don't know how they got the chance to— I think your father must have come upstairs while I was still sleeping and left the door wide open, or else I don't see how they managed it. They got to him before I could stop them."

The bird was folding in its wings now, sliding them down the wall, sluggishly.

"I'll just put him in the study again," I said calmly. "That would be the best thing. We can keep the doors closed and locked in there."

"Do whatever you want to, dear," she said in a rasping voice.

"Mama? You all right?"

"Just help the poor thing out."

It didn't struggle. It was exhausted by that point. As I picked it up it even seemed to cooperate with me, hunching, rounding itself like a buoy. It was warmer than I would have thought, underneath. And damper.

"Everything's under control, see, Ma?"

I slipped into one corner of the study, and lowered the Booby carefully onto a section of newspaper left there in the middle of the piles of magazines, thinking that might make it feel more secure, as if it were hunkered down surrounded by ledges, or rocks. The illusion must have worked, because after a minute or two its huge beak slowly closed, its eyes narrowed, and it dropped its head and seemed to fall asleep.

"Will you look at that?" I turned to her.

But Mama was nowhere in sight. I heard a bumping over my head—what sounded like an argument being finished. I stood and dropped down into my father's rollaway chair, shaking my head. Sighing. Another day, after this one. One more long day to go. My arms were tired, tingling, maybe from all the dog-wrestling, or maybe from the tug-of-war with Paul. I rested my elbows on my father's ink blotter, one of my hands sliding carelessly across his yellow notepad, accidentally backing over and curling its top, blank sheet. It's all right, chickadees, he had told us once when he'd caught us poring over his jottings and doodles and long graphs of dialogue. Go on and have a look. No one should be ashamed of how his thoughts appear straight out of the barrel.

In his lean hand he'd put down:

Water/Urine:

Wednesday in 40 ounces, out 20 ounces

Thursday

In 48, out 20

Friday—

In 48, out 20

Saturday—

WEIGHT GAIN
Wednesday, 197 lbs
Thursday, 198
Friday, 199
Saturday, 201

Symptoms:
Bloated feeling
Loss of appetite
Sleeplessness
Twitching
Coldness
Shortness of breath
Ischemia
Depression
Jeanie's concerns—
Pain, immobility
Isolation
Burden
Dissatisfaction
Loneliness
Dependence
Loss
Death

My eyes stayed glued to the bottom of the column. Underneath the last word my father had sketched, unmistakably, a hunting rifle.

I was up the stairs in three long steps, outside their bedroom. I heard noises like something being dragged, shoved into place.

"Come in," I heard Mama saying.

I made a point of opening the door calmly. My father sat, looking up at me from the edge of their half-made bed. Mama was dropping down beside him, bending over, unlacing one of her deck shoes, pulling it off. The chest in the corner had been pulled away from the wall, and its lid was thrown back. A pair of heavy blankets were piled up on the floor, next to it.

"What's going on?" I asked, casually.

"So you didn't go," my father said flatly.

"Where would I go?"

"You *said* you were."

Was it my imagination, or were the waves actually pounding against the legs of the house now, shaking it?

"Sarah and Paul went," I said.

"I know, son."

"They'll be fine, dear." Mama turned to him, and brushed some sand from the bedspread between them. "They have each other now."

My father kept on looking at me. "And what about you, son? No thought of giving in to nature's way, and settling down, and feathering a nest?"

I walked, carefully shrugging, over to the rocking chair. If ever there was a moment to make them feel heavy-handed, overwrought, melodramatic, this was it. I sat down, but so close to the front of the chair it nearly tossed me out of it.

"I don't feel all that desperate for it," I said when I was poised again, and looking at them steadily. "There's never any point in getting desperate."

Mama turned toward the darkened windows. "Dee, it's so misty out. Look. Almost . . . furry."

"Like it's getting our coats."

I hadn't eaten all day. I felt sick. I was dizzy. I had to concentrate, concentrate on keeping things together.

I gave up and blurted out, "I saw your notes. Down in your study. I'm not going to sit here and pretend I didn't. I know what you're both thinking."

"What are we thinking, son?"

"You're chickening out."

They stayed solemnly facing me, giving nothing away.

"How so, dear?"

"I'm not saying— I know it must be hard, for you, all this— I know it's what you've always talked about doing, going out with a bang, facing right into it. But don't you think it's—cowardice?"

"Not if you take it the right way, dear."

"I'd say you're taking it the wrong way, Mama."

"We'd planned," my father interrupted, "to have a chance to talk to both of you, this weekend. About all of this. But somehow, that didn't quite get organized. No, somehow it didn't quite work out."

"We thought you should each share some of the burden of discussion, dear. To be fair about it."

"But now, son . . ." He held his hands out. Deliberately helpless, I thought. "Looks like you're on deck solo. Looks like you're about to be given one rare opportunity."

"Oh, I don't know it's such an opportunity, Dee. There must be a thousand other things Harry would rather be doing on a Saturday night."

"You really think so?" My father raised his bushy white eyebrows. "You don't think most children wouldn't *jump* at a chance like this?"

I could feel panic rising, pushing against the thin cotton layer covering my chest. "You are not, seriously, going to rehearse this on me?"

"Not rehearse, dear. Scout?"

"And what about Sarah in all this?"

"We're hoping for the best there, dear. Hoping you can explain."

"Is it asking too much?" My father leaned forward from the edge of the bed. "We just need a chance to explain this calmly to one of you, Harry, so that you'll both understand. And we wanted to give you *some* chance to put your two cents in."

"We didn't want either of you to be taken off guard."

"We needed to explain that it's nothing personal. We don't want to leave you, but there just comes a point when you have to seize the reins of something before it gets out of hand. We're asking for your consideration."

Nothing personal. Out of hand. Consideration. My throat was so dry it hurt. "Why even bother asking? You're going to do what you want to, anyway. Aren't you? Isn't that what you're going to tell me, in the end, whenever you finally get around to it?"

"Well . . ." he acknowledged.

"We don't want to seem unreasonable to you, Harry."

They had given it a great deal of thought, they said. It was no hasty decision, nothing born out of a mood swing, or a fit of impatience, but a conscious conclusion, a revelation. They weren't in a hurry to die, no, but they weren't going to shy away from it either. It just seemed that if the darkness was going to come so soon in any case, but first bring with it so many unpleasantnesses that could be avoided, then the right thing to do was to beat it at its own game, and sprint *past* the finish. The only thing they had worried about was Sarah and me. Had we reached the point where it was possible for us to say, to admit, our parents deserved this?

"I don't know how you expect me to answer." The rocker wanted to tip like a scale underneath me.

"Say whatever's on your mind, dear."

"You're not in extremis? Are you? You're not catatonic, you're not on your backs, hooked up to anything, you're not eating out of a tube, not skeletons, wasted, like some I've known."

She misunderstood. Or misheard me. "That's true. We're in the best shape to take care of things right now."

"And if I say it, say, go on ahead, off yourselves, what am I? Have you thought about that? Either of you? What does that make me? What kind of person would that make me? And if I say no, don't go out while you still feel reasonably good, while you're still reasonably in control, what am I then? What would I be then?"

"It's not passing a sentence down on you!" my father objected quickly. "We take responsibility for what we decide. *We* decide."

"What is all this, then? This telling me?"

He ran his fingers through his hair until it was standing like an overturned root. He shrugged. Almost . . . sheepishly.

I blinked. "You want my approval."

"Understanding," he insisted.

"And why is that, Daddy? Why? Why do you think it would be so *important* to you, my approval?"

"Because—" He seemed momentarily stumped by this one. "It might make it easier?"

"For whom, Daddy?"

And here it was. All at once. The chance. My chance. They were sitting there quietly. Unsuspectingly. Waiting on me. And all I had to do, all I had to say, if I wanted to, was no. Hold it off from them. Keep it back. All this deep-down feeling. And wasn't that the proper thing to do, anyway—the *loving* thing? Keep all this feeling at bay? Wasn't that the way it had always been with us? No, I will not cooperate. I will not agree to let you hurt yourself in any way. That, after all, is my job.

I shook my head slowly at them. Watching them. They were wincing now, surprised—suddenly smaller, hunching on the tangled bed. I could hear the ocean outside striking, each bell indistinguishable from the last. I hate you, I hate you, I hate you. I wish you were dead, don't go, I wish you were dead. I want to be left alone, left alone, leave me alone, don't go, don't go, don't go.

In a flash, in a fleeting moment, so all out of proportion, I could send you, Mama, Daddy, both of you, without blessing to where there are no proportions. For not acknowledging the depths of desire, my desire, don't you see, don't you finally see it now—I could throw you out of all depths.

I had them. But I let them go. I let out a breath, changing course. "Can I just ask—when?"

Mama blinked. What had she glimpsed, I wondered. "We're still discussing that."

"Probably fairly soon, son," my father said.

"And can I ask—how?"

"It's a very private matter, dear. For the moment it's better you don't know, don't you think?"

"You're right. Of course you're right. I understand perfectly. I wouldn't want to have to brood over the details."

I had forgiven Timothy, too, after our last fight. We had kicked and tossed and knocked each other around, as usual, and then fucked, oblivious, like two truckers, and then after settling back, he'd nuzzled into my neck, unable to wind down completely, always so talkative. Dreaming, dreaming, going on and on about his plans, his schemes, his ideas, all the thoughts he boyishly, childishly believed were his own, and that no one else in the world had ever thought before. Wasn't it going to be fabulous? he confided in me. Weren't we going to do such wonderful things together, you and me, you and me, you writing more wonderful little bits of theater, me designing all the costumes, weren't we just going to do *amazing* things, Har, not just beautiful things but wildly gorgeous things, wicked things? He'd drummed his heels at the end of the mattress. You know, Harry, darling, it isn't just about doing something more beautifully than anyone else, it's all about doing the terrible things beautiful people think they're doing something terrible by getting close to.

In the middle of the night he'd woken up, wild, angry with me. He had dreamed it again, he said. He had, he *had.* That he was destined to design costumes and sets for some of my father's biggest and most brilliant Broadway plays. That he was bound to see their names permanently joined. It was his future, he said, and all of it could come true, it could—except that *I* stood in the way, me, I was like a giant brick wall in his way, refusing to introduce them, to make things happen. Why wouldn't I introduce them? What, what on earth was my problem? So selfish. So mean. Not everyone had such a helpful family background. Why couldn't I share?

But no, you don't share. Look at you. Look at you! You don't ever give me anything. Ever. You're so aloof, always looking down on me—how can I love you, love that? I can't love you. It's like getting my arms around a dam, you're impossible to love, you stand in the way of everything I deserve, everything I should be able to reach, there's nothing wrong with us using each other to get what we want, isn't that right? Except that you won't admit that, you can't admit the truth of things, you can't admit what I should rightly be, what I'm going to be, with or without you.

I'd shoved him out the door that same night. Then I'd gone into the bathroom and switched on the light. Opening up the medicine cabinet. He made a habit of keeping his sleeping pills in my apartment—sometimes it had been the only way he'd been able to calm down, to keep his body from flinching and flying around the room. Only a few, I thought to myself. Just enough so I can finally feel some real calm, a deep calm. Then I had run the bathtub and let the noise of the rushing drown out everything else.

I woke up in daylight, spewing. My arms were flailing. My hands had gone numb, and my feet, the bathwater was ice cold, I couldn't feel the porcelain underneath me. I was spurting water out my nose, thrashing like a baby, hauling myself over to one side and falling in a heap out of the tub, collapsed on the fur mat, grabbing a white towel from the ring over my head and wrapping it around my ears, trying to get warm. I couldn't stop shaking. I had to bite my nails to get the blood going again, to make certain of my extremities, that I had drawn everything back in from the edge. So. So this is how a beached whale feels, I thought, when I could think anything again at all. Uncertain what had been aimed for. Uncertain what had been meant.

The next feeling was embarrassment, flooding in. Looking down at my pinched nipples. At how close I had come to being . . . nothing.

And then the phone had rung. It was Mama.

· 21 ·

My father said, clearing his throat, "Nothing wrong with going downstairs now and catching the moon, just sitting for a little while out on the deck?"

Mama held her deck shoe up, studying it, like a cast she'd just taken off. "It'll be a pain getting this one back on. I'm so swollen."

"Leave it off then. No harm in bare feet, Jeanie."

I went on ahead of them. Everything was quiet; the dogs must have given up trying to scratch their way out into the hallway. At the bottom of the stairs, I waited. She appeared at the top, first, reaching for the wooden handrail. Then his bushy head emerged, over her right shoulder, his hand gripping her neck from above, leaning down hard on her as she took the steps one by one, following her, taking them slowly, carefully, too, both of them with their feet turned outward.

"I should check on the Booby," I remembered.

"We'll have to do something about him," Mama nodded. "And the dogs, too."

"Where is my bird?" my father asked.

"Behind your desk, Dad."

"Let's go in and see."

He pushed the French doors aside, his body cantilevering slightly, wavering, and switched on the light.

Mama started. "Oh dear. I think there's been some misunderstanding!"

The bird was nested in between the stacks of magazine pages. Rolled off to one side, halfway underneath her white breast, awkwardly—as though she didn't know what to do with it, now that it had arrived—was a pale blue-green egg.

"And probably more coming any minute," my father exhaled. "I remember that much from the book. It said one to three in a season."

"Dee? I'm not sure what to do at this point?"

"It doesn't make things different. Maybe only in the short term."

"I guess we really can't move it, though. Not for a little while, at least."

I stepped in. "I'll take care of it, don't worry. In the morning. I'll go and find a vet."

"Not on Sunday you won't, dear. Nothing's open here on Sundays."

"Well, what should we do in the meantime?" I asked.

"Come away, for now," Mama said. "Let's go out on the deck. And give this poor thing some privacy."

My father opened the sliding glass door. We stepped out together into the sticky night air.

"We want our ashes to be let loose right here, son."

"You won't get carried away very far then, Daddy."

"That's the whole idea. Our little bit for the sandbar."

I looked up. The stars were gathered in bunkers.

Mama leaned her elbows over the rail. "Harry, you'll bring someone nice out here, won't you? Someone special to you? One day? And there we'll both be, Dee, at the feet of those swimming boys."

"They'll end up walking all over us."

"Won't that be nice, now?"

"I think, Jeanie, strictly speaking, we won't feel anything. Just a guess."

"I don't know—Harry might." She tilted her chin back.

Listen, chickadees, just listen to those waves. It's the sound you hear when they bring you out from behind the curtain.

acknowledgments

Special thanks to Audrey Slate, and to the Texas Institute of Letters and the University of Texas at Austin for the gift of the Paisano Fellowship. Aimee Taub, Jennifer Hershey, Greg Michalson, Paul Chung, Laurel Doud, Debbie Wesselmann, Cynthia Mott, Gary Dressler, and Geoff and Simone Leavenworth have all helped this book on its way. Jane and Phil Mockford took me and my manuscript to higher ground—I am grateful still. To all the book club members who have invited my stories into their warm homes, warmest thanks, and, yes, you've got it, it is pronounced like the city in Italy. To my family, much love. For my husband, there can never be words enough. DMD